"I'm late!" Sabrina ✔ KT-511-990 who might be listening as she grabbed the doorknob. "Gotta go—"

THUNK!

Sabrina shrieked. Everything had gone black! And even worse—wet!

Bracing herself, Sabrina reached up to touch her head, hoping it was still there. But instead of skin, her fingertips touched smooth metal. "A bucket?"

The liquid drenching her was . . . *sniff, sniff* . . . "Fruit punch?"

This was no trick of the Other Realm—it was human trickery. Obviously someone had deliberately propped an old bucket of liquid over the door so that when she opened it, the bucket would fall and soak her. It was the oldest camp prank in the book.

"But who . . . ?" Sabrina dropped the bucket and strode to the steps, quickly glancing up and down the street looking for the culprit.

A rustle in the bushes caught her attention, and she dashed across the porch to look around the side of the house. She spotted what looked like the tip of a bushy brown tail disappearing through the bushes of the back garden.

Frustrated, and still wet and sticky, Sabrina stalked back to the front door. She was baffled. Who could have done this?

Titles in SABRINA, THE TEENAGE WTCH™ Pocket Books series:

All Pocket Books titles are available by post from:
Simon & Schuster Cash Sales, P.O. Box 29, Douglas, Isle of Man IM99 1BQ
Credit cards accepted. Please telephone 01624 836000,
Fax 01624 670923, Internet http://www.bookpost.co.uk
or email: bookshop@enterprise.net for details

Sabrina The Teenage Witch®

Fortune
Cookie Fox

Cathy East Dubowski

Based on Characters Appearing in Archie Comics

**And based upon the television series
Sabrina, The Teenage Witch
Created for television by Nell Scovell
Developed for television by Jonathan Schmock**

POCKET
B O O K S

LONDON · SYDNEY · NEW YORK

POCKET
B O O K S

An imprint of Simon & Schuster UK Ltd
Africa House, 64-78 Kingsway
London WC2B 6AH

A CIP catalogue record for this book is
available from the British Library

ISBN 0 671 02923 1

3 5 7 9 10 8 6 4 2

Printed by Caledonian International
Book Manufacturing,
Glasgow

Fortune
Cookie Fox

Chapter 1

Sabrina Spellman was late for school.

That shouldn't have been a problem for a teenage witch—who could wave her hand and, in less time than it takes to make microwave popcorn, instantly transport herself across town.

Or across the country.

Or across the universe.

Or even into the Other Realm—the world inhabited by witches, fairies, leprechauns, trolls, and myriad other magical beings.

(Actually, to do that she had to go through her aunts' personal portal to the Other Realm—the tiny towel-stacked linen closet in the upstairs hall of their old Victorian home. But it was just as fast.)

But the catch here was that Sabrina was only *half* witch and was being raised by her six-hundred-year-old aunts Zelda and Hilda. They were witches, like her father, and extremely doting. And extremely strict. And extremely involved with, and opinionated about, everything she did.

Which meant two important things.

One, they were mindful of her half-human side and wanted her to learn to live with grace and skill the life of a magical being in a mortal world.

And two, they thought it totally rude to use magic to clean up mistakes—like goofed-up spells and sleeping late.

So now she'd have to race to school with the speed of someone racing to get 'N Sync concert tickets. Otherwise known as teenage speed of light.

Sabrina threw back the covers, screeched to a stop in front of the full-length mirror on her closet door, and with a snap of her fingers selected "Way-Late Dress-Without-Thinking Outfit, Number 3": Flared jeans, light blue tank top with quarter-inch straps. After slinging her backpack over one shoulder, she zapped her mouth minty-fresh as she vaulted down the wooden stairs, conjured up an Egg McFluffin (witches can't do name brands), and aimed herself at the nearest exit.

"I'm late!" she shouted to anyone who might be listening as she grabbed the brass doorknob. "Gotta go—"

THUNK!

Sabrina shrieked.

Everything had gone black!

And even worse—wet!

Magic! Sabrina thought, her heart pounding in her chest. But was it the magic of friend or foe?

Bracing herself, Sabrina reached up to touch her head, hoping it was still there.

But instead of skin, her fingertips touched smooth metal. Frowning, she rapped the material with her knuckles.

Klung-g-g-g-g!

"Don't do that!" she told herself, wincing. Her head felt as if it were inside a bell.

Slowly, bracing for any magical side effects, she pulled the metal something off her head—it slid off easily—then held it out in front of her.

"A bucket?" It looked like a common, ordinary galvanized metal mop bucket.

The liquid drenching her was ... *sniff, sniff* ... "Fruit punch?"

Sabrina looked up. This was no trick of the Other Realm—it was human trickery. Obviously someone had deliberately propped an old bucket of liquid over the door, so that when she opened it, the bucket would fall and soak her.

It was the oldest camp prank in the book.

"But who ... ?" Shoving wet, sticky blond hair out of her face, Sabrina dropped the bucket and strode to the steps, glancing quickly up and down the street looking for the culprit.

Her neighbor Mrs. Neagle drove by in her new green minivan taking her kids to school. Sabrina waved to Kaity, Kristen, and little Sean buckled into the backseats.

I know it wasn't them, Sabrina thought as she watched the van turn at the corner. *They're way too nice.*

Then she heard someone running and quickly glanced the other way.

Nope. Just eighty-something Mr. Patton slowly jogging past in his EAT MY DUST T-shirt. *A little zany, but definitely not the prankster type.*

A rustle in the bushes caught her attention, and she dashed across the porch to look around the side of the house.

Nothing.

No wait—what's that . . . ? She spotted what looked like the tip of a bushy brown tail disappearing through the bushes of the back garden.

Sabrina sighed. Probably just a neighbor's dog taking a shortcut.

Frustrated, and still wet and sticky, Sabrina stalked back to the front door. She was baffled. Who could have done this?

Libby Chessler, her least favorite person at school, maybe?

Nah—Libby's the type who needs an audience for her acts of humiliation, Sabrina thought.

Besides, it probably wasn't sophisticated enough for Libby. It was such a lame prank, the kind kids pulled on each other at summer camp.

Sabrina's eyes narrowed. She knew only one person who had that kind of sick, juvenile humor. And he lived here—right under her own roof!

"Saaaa-lem!" she screeched, stomping into the front hall.

Two black ears popped up over the back of the couch in the living room. "Did someone call my name?" a black cat replied with a yawn.

Salem was no ordinary cat. He was an American shorthair—and darn proud of it! But he had also once been a fierce warlock—a warlock who tried to take over the world. Unfortunately he got caught, and the Witches' Council turned him into a cat for a hundred years. He lost all his powers—except one. The ability to talk.

Usually sarcastically.

"Uh, Sabrina," he said now, chuckling as he gazed at her dripping hair and clothes. "I believe you're supposed to get dressed *after* you take your shower—not before?"

"Very funny, Salem," Sabrina said through clenched teeth. "How *could* you?"

"How could I what?" Salem asked, surprised. But when he saw the serious look of menace on the face of the teenage witch—who still had *all* her powers—he quickly exclaimed, "Whatever it was— I'm innocent!"

"Yeah, right," Sabrina said. "I can't believe this! And I'm already late for school. Why, I ought to—"

"Meow!" Salem yowled as he ran toward the stairs.

"What is going on down here?" Aunt Zelda— slim, blond, and elegantly dressed in nice beige slacks and baby blue twinset sweater—pulled her reading glasses off as she glided down the stairs, a scholarly book in her hand.

Her younger sister Hilda followed, still wearing her worn MOZART ROCKS/'76 TOUR sleepshirt and fuzzy pink slippers. "Yeah," she mumbled sleepily, shoving a tangle of blond curls out of her half-opened eyes. "Didn't the Witches' Council make it illegal to be this noisy before noon?"

Salem leaped into the safety of Zelda's arms, knocking the book from her hand. "Help me!" he cried. "Sabrina's about to skin the cat!"

Sabrina lunged at Salem, but Zelda quickly turned and shoved him into Hilda's arms. "Hold it!" the oldest witch in the house commanded. "Will someone *please* explain to me what this is all about?"

"I'd be glad to!" Sabrina said, holding out her soggy arms. "Look what Salem did to me!" She explained how the bucket had fallen when she opened the door. "And I'm already going to be late for school!"

"I didn't do it!" Salem insisted.

Sabrina glared. "I don't believe you!"

Salem pretended to be deeply offended. "How can you doubt my word?"

All three witches glared at him. Salem would have blushed if his face weren't covered with thick black hair. "So . . . I've told a few fibs in my time," he said with a shrug. "But I never lie about important things." Salem leaped from Zelda's arms and padded toward Sabrina, careful to avoid the liquid pooling on the floor around her feet. "First of all, you know how I absolutely *loathe* water—"

"It's fruit punch," Sabrina pointed out.

Salem sniffed. "Yech! Disgusting! But that's even more proof. Nobody around here drinks this revolting beverage."

Sabrina crossed her arms. "So?"

Salem sputtered. "What—do you think I ran down to the corner Piggly Wiggly supermarket and purchased a jug of the stuff just so I could dump it on you?" He snorted. "I have better ways to spend my money."

Zelda's brows knit together in thought. "Hmm, good point, Salem."

"Thank you," he replied. "And besides, how in the world could I lift a heavy, fruit-punch-filled bucket and prop it up over the doorsill with these?" With all the drama of a courtroom lawyer, he sat back on his haunches and raised his tiny front paws in the air. "May I remind you, I am temporarily without the point-and-click skills you witches have at your disposal?"

Hilda whistled. "I think he's got you there, Sabrina."

Sabrina didn't want to admit it, but Salem's arguments made sense. She sighed in defeat. "Okay, I guess you're innocent."

Salem's whiskers twitched. "And . . . ?" he prompted.

Sabrina rolled her eyes. She hated being wrong. Even more humiliating was having to apologize to Salem, who could be absolutely obnoxious when he wanted to be. *"And . . . I'm sorry I falsely accused you of a crime, Salem."*

The black cat twitched his tail in satisfaction. "Apology accepted."

"Now that that's settled" —Zelda cleared her throat and glanced at the untidy floor—"would you mind mopping up, Sabrina dear?"

Sabrina sighed and snapped her fingers:

Handy mop,
Clean up this slop.

A mop blinked into existence and began swabbing up the tiny puddle on the floor. It reminded Sabrina of the mop in *The Sorcerer's Apprentice* scene in the movie *Fantasia.*

"Now to tidy up myself." Sabrina waved her hands in the air and said:

Soggy duds, hit the hamper,
Give me something a little less damp . . . er.

Aunt Zelda tsked.

"What? I'm in a hurry!" But Sabrina quickly waved her hand in the air, as if erasing something she'd written there, and tried again.

> *Off you go to the washer and dryer,*
> *You pitiful soggy wet clothes.*
> *I need some cool duds from the pages of*
> Teen People
> *So I'll be hip from my head to my toes."*

Sabrina's fruit-punch-soaked clothes instantly disappeared, replaced so quickly by a new outfit that you couldn't even see her underwear. Her outfit—a short, but not too short, light blue slip dress with hand-painted yellow daisies—was definitely a knockout. So were the chunky black slides. Next she zapped some spring water through her hair to rinse, then snapped her fingers.

A blow dryer and hairbrush hovered in the air. With a wave of her hands, the two commenced a duet of drying and styling Sabrina's soggy hair.

When they finished their task, Sabrina glanced into the antique mirror that hung in the entry hall. Her hair looked sleek and shiny. She'd definitely have to add this to her regular wardrobe.

"There now, that's better," Zelda said, smiling. "Everything's back to normal."

"But it's not," Sabrina insisted.

"Yeah, you missed a spot!" Salem told the mop, pointing with his paw.

But Sabrina shook her head. "No, you don't understand. What I mean is, I still don't know who played that prank on me. Do you think it could have been a neighborhood kid? Or maybe somebody from school?"

"Well, let's see now," Zelda said. "Let's try to determine when our culprit may have set up the prank. None of us has used that door since suppertime last night—"

"Well, not exactly," Hilda interrupted, blushing a little. "I did. I came through it about midnight."

"What?" Zelda exclaimed. "But I thought you went to bed early last night to read."

Hilda looked puzzled. "Where'd you get that idea?"

"From you," Zelda said. "You said you were going to spend the evening with *The Count of Monte Cristo!*"

"I did," Hilda replied. "I had a date with him."

"But, Hilda," Zelda sputtered, "the Count of Monte Cristo isn't a real person, he's a fictional character created by Alexandre Dumas in 1844!"

Hilda made a face. "I know that—*now,* Miss Smartypants." She kicked at the floor with her fuzzy pink slippers and mumbled, "Last time I use *that* dating service."

"So why didn't you just use the linen closet when you came home?" Zelda asked.

"I didn't want to wake the rest of you up," Hilda explained. When the Spellmans entered or exited their linen-closet portal to the Other Realm, the house shook with thunder and lightning.

"Hilda, really, you—"

"Aunt Zelda! Aunt Hilda! What about me?"

"Sorry, dear," Aunt Zelda said. "We'll talk about this later," she told her sister.

"Who set me up with this prank?" Then she snapped her fingers. "I know who it was! Cousin Amanda."

Zelda shook her head. "I don't think so."

"Why not?" exclaimed the portrait hanging on the wall. The painting of Aunt Louisa—a stern-looking woman with her dark hair pulled back into a prim bun, a high lacy collar at her throat—gave new meaning to the expression, "If walls could talk." Unlike the paintings in most mortal homes, this one could come to life and suddenly jump into the conversation, which could be quite startling at times. It had taken Sabrina months to get used to it and to learn *not* to use the kitchen phone for private conversations. Aunt Louisa was quite a snoop.

"That Amanda! She's the brattiest little witch in the cosmos!" Aunt Louisa huffed indignantly. "Why, the last time she was here, she drew a mustache on me!"

Sabrina agreed with Aunt Louisa. Once, when Sabrina lost her mind and agreed to babysit for her, Amanda turned Sabrina into a cute little doll. Then she locked her in a toy box along with other toys and stuffed animals who used to be people before they did something the little witch didn't like.

But Aunt Zelda shook her head as she approached Sabrina. "I spoke with Cousin Marigold yesterday and it seems Amanda has the bat pox. It's kind of like chicken pox, very contagious," she explained to Sabrina. "She's been in quarantine for a week already and has at least another two to go."

"Then who could it be?" Sabrina whined.

"Hmmm," Salem purred, his whiskers twitching. "How do you know for sure that the prank was aimed at you?"

Sabrina shook her head. "What do you mean?"

"Well, anyone could have gone out that door first thing this morning," Salem said. "Even—even m-m-m-me!" His eyes widened and he shivered as he imagined what it would have been like to be drenched in sticky pink liquid as he stepped out onto the porch in search of his morning *Wall Street Journal.*

"You know, Sabrina, Salem's right," Aunt Zelda said. "Maybe you're not the target. Maybe it was simply a random prank."

"Yeah, some brainless kids get their jollies doing dumb tricks like that," Aunt Hilda said. She walked over to the bay window and glared outside. "Let me take care of it."

"Now, Hilda," Aunt Zelda admonished, "we don't need any more frogs in the neighborhood."

Hilda pouted. "All right." Then she brightened. "How 'bout I just give them a bad case of athlete's foot?"

"Ohmygosh!" Sabrina suddenly said. "I almost

12

forgot—I am *so* beyond late! Oh, Aunt Zelda, pleasepleaseplease let me zap myself to school this morning? It wasn't my fault I got soaked."

Zelda smiled. "Sure, sweetheart. Go ahead. Oh—and here." She zapped a small white envelope into Sabrina's hand.

"What's this?" Sabrina asked.

"A note from your legal guardian," Zelda said with a smile, "in case you need an excuse for being late."

"Thanks!" Sabrina said and gave her aunt a hug. "You're the best. And I promise, I'll be up at the crack of dawn tomorrow."

"We'll see," Zelda said dryly.

Sabrina grabbed her backpack from the front porch, then came back inside.

> *One plus one is always two,*
> *Two plus two is always four—*
> *Zap me to a hidden spot*
> *Just outside the school's front door.*

"Bye!" she said, waving to her aunts, just before she disappeared like an image deleted from a video.

"Your meter's improving!" Aunt Zelda called after her. The poetry of spells didn't have to scan or rhyme perfectly to work, but Zelda encouraged it as a sign of a more accomplished magic.

Sabrina's aunts wandered into the kitchen and sat down at the breakfast table. Lost in thought, Zelda zapped them a healthy breakfast of oat bran granola with skim milk, fresh-squeezed orange juice, and black decaffeinated tea.

Frowning, Hilda swirled her finger and—*zap!*—converted the breakfast into a fresh-baked gooey coffee cake and a double latté with extra cream. She waited for her big sister to protest. To lecture. To change it all back into something more nutritional.

But Zelda did nothing. She just sat there, stirring her spoon around and around in her coffee, staring into space.

Frowning, Hilda conjured up additional calories and sugar—a huge plateful of little white-powdered doughnuts. Then sat back and waited for her sister to freak.

Zelda didn't even notice!

"Zel!" Hilda exclaimed, her frown changing into a look of real concern. "Speak to me! What's wrong?"

Zelda sighed and turned to her sister. "This prank . . ."

"What about it?"

"It has me worried."

Hilda gasped. "You mean you don't think it was just some punks practicing random acts of rudeness?"

"I don't know," Zelda murmured worriedly as she absentmindedly reached for a little powdered doughnut. "But perhaps we should keep our eyes open. Just in case."

Chapter 2

"Ouch!" Sabrina appeared at Westbridge High School seconds later in a hidden space all right: a stand of very scratchy bushes just beneath a classroom window near the front of the school.

Okay, so maybe the poetry of my spells is improving. Still gotta work on my geography skills.

Just then she heard a window being raised above her head.

She froze, not wanting to draw attention to herself hiding in the bushes on school property.

Splash!

Not again! Sabrina silently moaned.

Someone (a teacher?) had apparently opened the window to empty a vase of faded flowers. The smelly water and wilted blossoms and stems couldn't have hit Sabrina more squarely if the person had purposely aimed for her nose.

The window slammed closed and Sabrina

groaned as she peeked out of the bushes. The schoolyard was empty; the final bell must have rung. Sabrina raised her hand to point herself clean when she heard—

"Eww."

Sabrina winced as she looked into the horrified brown eyes of Libby Chessler, Westbridge High's head cheerleader and self-appointed Queen of the Universe. She smoothed her own perfectly blow-dried long black hair and stared at Sabrina as if she were some kind of swamp thing.

At the moment Sabrina had to admit she did sort of smell like one.

"What *are* you doing?" the cheerless cheerleader said in a way only the self-appointed president of the Cool Club could demand.

"I was, uh . . ." Sabrina struggled for an excuse, ". . . just, uh . . . looking for—"

"Never mind—*freak.*" Libby turned to a girl whom Sabrina had just noticed standing behind her. The girl was strikingly beautiful, with long black hair that nearly reached her waist, dark brown eyes, and a slim delicate figure. She must be a new girl at Westbridge High. Sabrina was sure she'd never seen her before.

"First lesson in an American high school, Mei," Libby informed the girl, "avoid freaks like Sabrina."

"Freaks?" the girl asked in a voice lightly brushed with a Chinese accent.

"Students who do not meet our standards of

cool," Libby explained. She breezed past Sabrina toward the front steps of the school, her head averted as if from the scene of a disaster. "I don't know what she's up to, and I *really* don't want to know, but we need to leave before it rubs off on us."

Aunt Hilda's idea—a raging case of athlete's foot—came to mind, but Sabrina squelched the urge. She'd already turned Libby into a pineapple and a goat. In the long run, it only caused more trouble. Something she didn't need more of right now.

Libby grabbed the new girl by the arm and pulled her up the stairs.

Mei met Sabrina's eyes and gave her a half smile.

Sabrina smiled back. Maybe Mei was nice, even though she was hanging out with Libby. Maybe she was too new to know how low Libby could be.

Sabrina waited till the girls disappeared into the school, did a quick wash and dry on her smelly hair and clothes, then hurried up the front steps and through the school's heavy front doors. Hugging the walls, she hurried toward her locker. Up ahead she saw Libby waltzing confidently down the hall, seemingly fearless of getting caught coming into the school late. Mei walked quietly behind her. But just as the girls passed the office, Vice Principal Kraft stepped out into the hall.

Sabrina grinned. *Now Libby will get it.*

But the cheerleader didn't flinch. "Hi, Mr. Kraft," she sang out, as cheerfully as if they'd met on a Sunday in the park.

"Well, good morning, Libby," the vice principal replied. He hesitated a moment, then said, "Aren't we a little, teensy-weensy bit late this morning?"

Libby shot the man a look that ancient queens might have found useful to put peasants in their place. "Aren't we a little bit *balding* this morning?" she replied.

And as Mr. Kraft hurried into his office to check the status of the slight balding spot on the back of his head, Libby winked at Mei and dragged her down the hall toward class.

I can't believe it! Sabrina thought. *But at least she did me a favor, getting Mr. Kraft out of the way.* Sabrina scurried to her locker, dropped her heavy backpack to the floor, then spun the combination lock on her locker. When it clicked open, she pulled open her locker and—

Whoosh!

Sabrina stared.

Now, that is weird.

An avalanche of white popcorn tumbled out of her locker and spilled across the scuffed linoleum floor.

Sabrina shook her head in disbelief, *"Where did that come from?"* She had no idea.

But she knew one thing. She'd better get rid of it—fast.

She raised her finger and opened her mouth to pronounce a quick unpop-the-popcorn spell—

Crunch!

—then froze when she heard someone crunch to a stop behind her. She peeked over her shoulder.

Vice-Principal Kraft. *Who else?*

"Sabrina Spellman," Mr. Kraft scolded. "You know it's against the rules to snack in the halls during school hours." He whipped out his little notebook and began to scribble with a small, slightly chewed Number 2 pencil.

"But, Mr. Kraft—" Sabrina began.

"Don't." The vice principal held up his hand. "Don't try to explain, excuse, deny, lie, or weasel out of it. I've heard it all and I'm immune to it." He peered at her over his glasses. "Just clean it up."

He flipped his notebook closed, slipped it into his inside suit-coat pocket, then started to walk away. Three steps down the hall, he froze, then pivoted.

The notebook came back out. "Oh, yes. And you're late as well," he announced.

"I, uh—" The note! Sabrina dug into her backpack and pulled out the note Aunt Zelda had written her. "I have a note," she said proudly. She handed him the small white envelope.

Mr. Kraft plucked it from her hands with distaste. "You know I do not accept excuses for lateness," he reminded her. But then the delicate feminine handwriting on the front of the envelope froze him. Melting before Sabrina's eyes, the man reverently slipped open the envelope. As he read the lines inside, his face softened, for he had once had a crush on Aunt Zelda. He shook his head. "How such a

19

lovely lady could have such a late niece I can't imagine. Okay, Sabrina, I'll look the other way, just this once. Now, clean up this mess and get to class!"

He carefully refolded the note and started to slip it into his pocket next to his notebook—and his heart.

"Um, could I have that back, please?" Sabrina asked. "I need it to show my first-period teacher."

Mr. Kraft scowled, but returned the note. With that he went off in search of other students to torment.

Relieved, Sabrina turned back to the popcorn.

It wasn't April Fools' Day. It wasn't her birthday. Who could have done this? And why? Filling someone's locker full of popcorn was kind of a weird thing to do. Was it supposed to be mean? Or just funny?

And did it have anything to do with this morning's prank with the bucket?

Sabrina checked inside her locker and felt around in the popcorn on the floor, searching for some kind of clue. But there was absolutely no sign of who might have done this. Mortal or supernatural creature? One thing was for sure, she'd better clean up fast and get to class. She raised her finger and—

"Whoa, Sabrina, what happened?"

Sabrina smiled at Harvey Kinkle—the boy with the puppy-dog eyes who made her pulse pop like popcorn. Normally she'd be delighted to see him, but not when she wanted some privacy for a little quick magic.

"Hi, Harvey."

Harvey looked around at the popcorn spilling across the floor. "Is this your science project?"

Sabrina chuckled. "No." Then she peered closely at Harvey. He'd appeared suddenly out of nowhere. Could he possibly have stuffed the popcorn in her locker as some kind of affectionate surprise? "Harvey," she said, "come on, tell me the truth, did you do this?"

Harvey looked totally taken aback, and quite alarmed. "No!"

Sabrina sighed and instantly believed him. Harvey was a wonderful guy—sweet and kind and fun—but he was definitely not the devious type. He was about as honest and trustworthy as a golden retriever—which, actually, he'd been for a week once when Sabrina's magic misfired and switched Harvey's body with Macdougal, a dog Harvey had been pet-sitting. "I didn't think so," she reassured him. "But I wish I knew who did." She didn't tell him about the bucket of fruit punch.

"Maybe it was a Secret Pal," Harvey said. "Or someone who wanted to surprise you." He suddenly looked horrified. "It's not your birthday, is it?"

"No," Sabrina said. "You know my birthday's near the beginning of school."

Harvey looked relieved. "Oh, yeah. I just got worried there for a minute." He scooped up a handful of popcorn and shoved some into his mouth. "Mmm! At least it's the good stuff. Do you want me to help you put it back in your locker?"

Sabrina laughed. "Uh, I don't think so, Harv. I just need to clean it up." Then she frowned at him. "What are you doing wandering the halls anyway? Mr. Kraft's on the prowl with his little notebook and pencil."

Harvey held up a little wooden rectangle. "I've got a hall pass. "Coach got me out of first period so I could go get my weight checked with the school nurse. But she's not in." He glanced at the big round clock across the hall. "I have plenty of time."

Sabrina smiled at Harvey, then blinked at her locker. "Oh, look here," she said, reaching in. "I just happen to have a great big trash bag." She unfolded the bag and got down on her knees with Harvey. Their hands met as they reached for the same scoop of popcorn.

He smiled at her. She smiled at him.

Sometimes, Sabrina reminded herself, *magic can get in the way.* Using magic, she could clean up all this popcorn in about three seconds flat. But there were a lot worse things than spending first period picking up popcorn the *mortal* way with the adorable Harvey Kinkle.

"Did you meet her?" Sabrina's best friend Valerie exclaimed as they stood together in the school lunch line. "She's *so, so* nice. She's living with

Libby, but she doesn't look at me like I'm some kind of disgusting bug. You know what I mean?"

Sabrina reached for a Sloppy Joe, then decided it looked a little too sloppy and put it back.

"Hey, you can't put that back!" the lunch lady hollered. "You touch it, you eat it."

"Nice slogan," Sabrina mumbled, returning the plate to her tray. "Who are you talking about?" she asked Valerie.

"Mei!" Valerie exclaimed.

Mei. The girl she'd seen with Libby this morning.

"I saw her once this morning, but I haven't met her," she said, looking to see if any of the vegetables looked edible. "I haven't had any classes with her yet. And what do you mean, she's living with Libby?"

"Oh, haven't you heard?" Valerie said, reaching for the fried baloney and sauerkraut casserole. "She's a new exchange student from someplace in China. She's living with Libby's family for the rest of the year! Isn't that exciting? I'd love to have an exchange student live at my house."

"That's weird," Sabrina said as they neared the end of the line. "It's the middle of the semester. Exchange students usually come for the whole year."

Valerie shrugged as they carried their food to the regular table in the middle of the Twilight Zone— the vague region between the geek tables and the popular tables and the athlete tables. "I guess she was delayed arriving here for some reason. Maybe they're on a different calendar because of Chinese New Year's."

Sabrina didn't think that had anything to do with it, but before she could pursue it, she noticed that a crowd had gathered around a table in the popular region of the cafeteria. "What's going on over there?"

Valerie stood up to look. "I don't know. I can't see. There are too many people." She sat down with a look of resignation on her face. "Just some fun activity that I got left out of, as usual, I guess."

Just then Harvey emerged from the group and came over to sit down with Sabrina and Valerie. He had a dazed-looking expression on his face, and in his hand he held a tiny paper figure as if it were made of glass.

"Whatcha got, Harvey?" Sabrina asked as she tried to pick up her sloppy Sloppy Joe.

"It's called origami," Harvey said breathlessly as he laid the paper creature on the table. He propped his chin on his folded arms to admire it. "It's a tiny little frog. Mei made it for me by folding paper. She is *so* nice! Look!" He pressed down on the little figure, then removed his finger—and the little paper frog hopped in the air.

"Whoa!" Harvey exclaimed with a huge grin. "Isn't that just the coolest thing you ever saw?"

"That is *so* cool," Valerie agreed.

Harvey's eyes left the tiny paper frog only long

enough to gaze at Mei with a look that Sabrina would have preferred he save for her. "Isn't she neat?"

Sabrina's heart twisted just a little to hear him praise the beautiful new girl. *Don't go there,* she lectured herself. *You know how Harvey feels about you.*

"She promised to teach me how to do it," Harvey added.

"Do what?"

Harvey pointed at his frog. "This origami stuff."

"Do you think she'd teach me, too?" Valerie asked hopefully.

"Oh, yeah, I'm sure she would," Harvey said. "She is—"

"So nice," Sabrina chimed in. She was getting a little sick of hearing how nice Mei was. Suddenly a thought crossed her mind. "Hey, I thought origami was a traditional *Japanese* craft."

"So?" Valerie said, a hint of challenge in her voice. "Maybe they do it in China, too. Besides, who cares? She does it and it's cool. You don't have to be from a particular country to do their tradition-al craft."

"Sorry." Sabrina took a bite of her Sloppy Joe and looked back across the room. Through a gap in the crowd she could see Mei smiling as she fash-ioned the little figures out of paper. Cool kids and geeks alike surrounded Mei like moths around a flame. Like kids around a rap star. Libby sat beside her with a satisfied grin, as if showing off a new puppy who could do tricks, as if she somehow deserved credit for bringing this delightful new person to the masses.

Why does it bug me? Sabrina wasn't sure.

Then Mei looked up and caught Sabrina staring at her. She smiled at her again, that same Mona Lisa half smile she'd bestowed on her that morning when Libby had been mean to her. Sabrina suddenly felt ashamed for harboring bad feelings about her. She *did* seem really nice.

But maybe that was the weird part. Niceness didn't usually make you popular at Westbridge High School.

Of course, being beautiful doesn't hurt, a little voice inside her head said.

"Shut up," she muttered to the little voice.

Harvey and Val stared at her.

"What did you say?" Harvey asked.

"Oh! Uh, I . . . nothing," she muttered. She stirred her green-flecked mashed potatoes. Ick. The cafeteria ladies had a habit of stirring scallions into everything. They seemed to think it was some kind of cute display of school spirit because of a typo a few years ago that had turned the Westbridge High School *Fighting Stallions* into the *Fighting Scallions*. It took a lot of self-restraint not to use her magic to turn the mashed potatoes into a frozen-yogurt sundae. "So, guys, what are we doing this weekend?"

But neither friend answered. Each was too busy smiling as Mei came over to their table.

"Hi!" Mei said, flicking her shining dark hair over her shoulder.

"Hi," Valerie said, beaming.

"Everybody loves your frog," Harvey said, stumbling to his feet. He grinned from ear to ear as he held up the little creature.

"I'm *so* glad," Mei replied. "It gives me great pleasure to share my talent."

"That is *so* nice," Val gushed.

Sabrina tried not to roll her eyes. But she couldn't help but notice how well Mei spoke English, with only a hint of an accent—just enough to make her sound attractively exotic.

"Um, this is our friend Sabrina," Valerie said.

"*Sa-BRI-na,*" Mei said softly, drawing out the syllables as if examining a long silk scarf. "What a lovely name." She laughed lightly, a sound like water trickling over rocks in a brook. "We met already, this morning. Didn't we, *Sa-BRI-na?*"

Sabrina nodded, blushing a little, waiting for her to say something about the state she'd been in— hiding in the bushes drenched in rank flower water—when she and Libby found her.

But Mei simply smiled her Mona Lisa smile again.

That was nice of her, Sabrina thought. Then, *Oooh! Now I'm calling her nice! If I hear the word* nice *one more time—*

"Nice outfit," Harvey said admiringly.

Sabrina nearly choked. Harvey rarely noticed clothes. Sure, he complimented Sabrina if she was dressed up for a dance or other special event. But normally, he wouldn't be able to tell whether the outfit she was wearing was brand new or something she'd worn for three days in a row.

Sabrina had to admit Mei did look great in the clothes she was wearing—a clingy pale pink spaghetti-strap top over a short black skirt and black stacked shoes. In fact, extremely cool for a girl who'd just arrived in the States from China. Maybe she was from a big city?

"Where exactly are you from?" Sabrina blurted out.

Harvey and Valerie stared at her as if she had just said something totally rude.

"Oh, a little village in the north," Mei said. Then she turned to Harvey and laid a hand on his arm.

"Which one?" Sabrina persisted. *Why am I doing this?* she asked herself. "My aunt Zelda knows a lot about China. Maybe I know it."

"Oh, it's so small, I'm sure none of you has ever heard of it," Mei said, her hand still on Harvey's arm.

"Try me."

Mona Lisa smiled again.

"Since when did you become so interested in geography?" Val said with an embarrassed laugh.

"Hey, isn't that what exchange students are all

about?" Sabrina said lightly. "Exchanging information about where they come from?"

"I would be glad to tell you about my homeland," Mei said. "Sometime when I have more time. But now" —she looped her arm through Harvey's and stared up into his eyes— "I think we have a class to go to. Harvey, would you mind helping me find my way?"

"Sure, glad to," Harvey said politely.

Sabrina was definitely not liking this.

Especially when he simply turned and began walking away with Mei, without even a "See you later, Sab."

Chapter 3

I *wonder what the secret scientific formula for popularity is,* Sabrina thought in science that afternoon as kids gathered around Mei and Libby's lab table.

Their teacher had just announced that the class should choose partners to work on a research project.

Sabrina sighed. At least Harvey wasn't in this class. He'd probably be in line to be Mei's partner, too. Then she'd never see him. It seemed that Harvey had volunteered to be Mei's tour guide for the rest of the day, week, or century. Whenever she'd seen him since lunch, he'd been listening intently to something Mei was saying and didn't even see her.

I am not jealous, she kept repeating to herself. Maybe if she said it enough times, she could make it true.

An idea occurred to her. Maybe if she used a little magic, she could hook Mei up with some other eager male volunteer. Then she could go back to being the one to hang onto Harvey's arm.

But who? Everyone seemed crazy about Mei. She glanced at her lab partner, Mark Wong. He was Asian-American. Maybe he and Mei would have a lot in common.

She got up and went to the pencil sharpener and inserted her already-sharpened pencil. Her aunts always warned her against interfering in the lives of mortals. *But this is an emergency!* she reasoned. Slowly turning the crank, she whispered:

> *Test tube, beaker, DNA,*
> *Make Mark and Mei partners right away!*

She smiled, then hurried back to her seat at her lab table, where Mark sat, doodling on his notes. Sabrina smiled at him, waiting for him to get up and go connect with Mei.

Nothing happened.

She glanced over at Mei.

Hmm, my spell was kind of vague. Maybe she's gonna come over here and ask him.

Nope.

Sabrina was getting impatient. "Hey, Mark," Sabrina finally asked. "Do you have a lab partner yet?"

Mark looked up at her with an eager smile. "Not yet."

"Great!" She laid a hand on his arm. "Why don't you go ask Mei?"

Mark gave her a look. "I'm not interested."

Huh? Not interested? If Mark wasn't interested, he was probably the only boy in school who wasn't. He'd have to have magic powers to resist the dazzling exchange student's charm. For that matter, how could he resist Sabrina's spell? "How come?" she asked him. "I mean, everybody says she's really, really nice. And she's from China. Maybe you guys could go out."

"Hey," Mark snapped. "Do you, like, want to date everybody who's from the United States?"

Sabrina blushed. "Sorry," she said. "I didn't mean it like—"

"Don't worry about it," Mark said, the sharpness gone from his voice. "I know what you meant." He shrugged. "But I'm more interested in you."

Sabrina looked at him.

"Uh, I mean—you know, to work on the project." Now it was Mark's turn to blush.

Sabrina sighed, staring at Mei. Something was definitely short-circuiting her magic. Maybe a solar flare or a windstorm on Jupiter. Or maybe it was just her lousy mood that was throwing off her magic. Hey, she was only human. Half human, that is.

"So, do you want to?" Mark asked.

Sabrina snapped her attention back to Mark. "Do I want to what?"

"Be my partner. For the project."

"Sure. Why not?" She glanced across the room. "Looks like everyone else is paired up with Mei."

"It is normal to be interested in something new."

Sabrina laughed. "That sounds like a fortune in a fortune cookie."

Mark nodded, pretending to be serious. "Much wisdom comes from eating cookies."

Sabrina laughed. How come she'd never noticed before how funny Mark was? She guessed it was because he was usually kind of quiet—not the class clown type at all. But being his partner for the project could be lots of fun. "So, do you think we could somehow work cookies into our project?"

"Couldn't hurt to try!"

Exactly, Sabrina thought. And it couldn't hurt to try to forget about Mei.

The teacher called the class to order and took down everyone's lab partner. Libby insisted on having Mei for herself, acting as if it were some sort of prize she was entitled to.

They spent the first twenty minutes discussing possible topics for projects, then worked an experiment using the microscopes.

"Do you want to look first?" Sabrina asked Mark.

"No, you go ahead. Tell me what you see, and I'll write it down."

Sabrina leaned her head down to the microscope and adjusted the eyepiece so she could see. But she didn't see anything. Was the slide in right?

"What do you see?" Mark prompted.

Sabrina sat up. "I don't see anything."

Mark just stared at her. Across the aisle, someone giggled. Faces turned toward her, and laughter rippled across the classroom. Soon the whole class was looking at her and laughing. She heard Libby's laugh above all the others.

Sabrina glanced around, trying to catch the joke. "What's so funny?"

That sent everyone into a new burst of laughter. Even Mark was trying not to laugh.

Then suddenly Mei was at her side. "Here," she said, handing Sabrina a pack of tissues and a small mirror from her bag. "Your eye," she said with a curious frown. "It has something on it."

Sabrina grabbed the mirror and peered at herself. A big circle of black circled her eye—like a trick black eye. Obviously someone had blackened the eyepiece of the microscope for a joke. But who had done it? And when? Did someone in the last class do it, not knowing who would be sitting here? Or was the joke intended for her?

Sabrina tried to laugh, too, to hide her embarrassment.

"Hey, Sabrina," Libby joked. "I think you're overdoing it with the eyeliner. Maybe you should get a makeover at the mall." Her friends tittered.

"Libby's right," Mark said.

Sabrina was stunned. Mark was agreeing with Libby's taunts?

"Way too much black." He took the tissue from her hand and dabbed gently at her eye, trying to wipe away the black smudge. "But you don't need any makeup at all. You're beautiful just the way you are."

Sabrina blushed at the compliment, but Mark's kind words seemed to take the wind out of the joke. The laughter died and her classmates turned back to their work.

"Thanks, Mark," Sabrina whispered.

"No problem," he said with a shrug. "Can't let Libby have the last word in these things, now, can we?" He looked away and began to clean the eyepiece with the tissue.

Yes, Sabrina thought as she looked at her new lab partner. *I've definitely underestimated this guy.*

After the last class of the day Sabrina hurried to try to catch Harvey at his locker. He was just clicking his lock shut when she got there.

"Hi, Sabrina."

"Harvey, hi. I'm glad I caught you. I heard they canceled practice this afternoon. So I was hoping we could walk home together. Maybe stop at the Slicery for something to eat."

Harvey shifted his book bag on his shoulder. "Sorry, Sab. I . . . kind of made other plans."

Sabrina's shoulders slumped. "Gotta babysit for your little sister again?"

"Not exactly."

Sabrina waited for him to say more, but just then Mei appeared at his side. "Ready, Harvey?"

Harvey grinned. "Ready."

Mei gave Sabrina her Mona Lisa smile. "Libby has a dentist appointment this afternoon, so Harvey offered to show me around Westbridge. Isn't that nice?"

"Nice," Sabrina said through a tight smile. "Very nice."

"Maybe you could take me to that place called the Slicery that I keep hearing about," Mei said with a big smile. "All the kids say the food there is the best."

"Sure," Harvey said. "It's a great place. You'll love it."

Sabrina waited a moment, hoping Harvey might ask her to come along, too, since she'd just suggested going there herself. But he didn't, and then she was glad, because she wasn't sure she wanted to go there with him and Mei anyway.

She took a few steps backward, her smile feeling awfully tight and forced. "Well, I'll see you two *nice* folks later." Then she turned and hurried down the hall toward the school's front entrance. Sabrina was a pretty tough cookie, but she didn't want to see Harvey and Mei walk off arm in arm.

Sabrina watched her step all the way home.

Nothing weird happened.

She walked up the steps to her front porch and carefully opened the door.

Nothing spilled on her.

She went to her room and sat down on her bed.

No whoopee cushion announced itself.

She looked under her bed.

No surprises.

She jumped up and ran to her closet and looked inside.

Nothing sprang out at her or fell onto her head.

"Is this a solitary game, or can two play?" Salem finally purred from his sunny spot on the windowsill.

Sabrina nearly shrieked. "Salem! I didn't see you. How long have you been there?"

"The whole time you've been in here acting weird," he said with a grin.

Sabrina flopped down on her bed and let out a long sigh. "I was looking out for practical jokes." She told him about the ones that happened at school. "But nothing's happened to me for the last" —she checked her watch—"fifty-seven minutes. I hope that's a good sign."

Salem flicked his tail. "I'll keep my paws crossed for you."

"Where are Aunt Zelda and Aunt Hilda?" she asked.

"The Other Realm Better Business Bureau," Salem replied. "Zelda's trying to help Hilda get her money back from that bogus dating service. They said to tell you they'd be home late."

"No problem. I've got lots of homework." She

zapped herself a few slices from the Slicery, including a slice with anchovies for Salem. But then, just as Salem pounced, she zapped them back to the restaurant. Thinking about the Slicery made her feel too miserable.

"Pffft!" Salem complained spitting out the mouthful of bedspread he'd just bitten into. "Where'd my anchovies go?"

"Sorry, Salem." Sabrina pointed him up a can of anchovies.

Salem pawed at the unopened tin. "Didn't anyone ever tell you it's not nice to tease your cat?"

"What?"

Salem shoved the can toward her. "An *opened* can might be even tastier."

"Oh, sorry, Salem. I guess I've just got my mind on other things." She magically zipped open the can, then opened her notebook to look up the night's assignments. Maybe a few hours of math, science, and verb conjugations would keep her busy—too busy to think about Harvey and Mei having a good time at what used to be her and Harvey's favorite place.

She studied all afternoon. She and Salem made tacos for dinner and ate them in front of the TV while making fun of all the infomercials. Then Salem went to sleep.

Bored, Sabrina called Valerie just to talk. Her best friend could usually cheer her up when she was feeling sorry for herself.

Val's mother answered the phone. "I'm sorry, Sabrina. Valerie's not home right now."

"Oh. Do you know when she'll be home?" Sabrina asked.

"I'm not sure. She was going to the library, then she was supposed to meet Harvey and . . . I forget her name . . . the new exchange student . . ."

"Mei," Sabrina supplied.

"Yes. Well, she was supposed to meet them at the mall for dinner at the food court. I'm not sure when she'll be back. Would you like to leave a message?"

"No, thanks. No message." She hung up and stared into space. *So my boyfriend and my best friend are out having a good time with Mei. Without me.*

She tried not to let it make her feel bad. But sometimes not even magic was powerful enough to stop your feelings from getting hurt.

She watched a little more TV with Salem snoring in her ear from his perch on the back of the couch. Then she went up to her room and got ready for bed. She changed her clothes, brushed her teeth, and slipped under the covers.

As soon as her feet reached the bottom, she screamed and jumped out of bed. *"Ewww!"*

A sleepy-looking Salem bolted into her room from downstairs. "Who? What? Sabrina, are you all right?"

"Something—something's in my bed!" she squealed.

Salem poised on the pillow ready to attack—or flee—if necessary as Sabrina bravely yanked back the covers.

Sabrina couldn't believe what she saw.

"Gummi worms!"

About a pound of the colorful, wiggly, jiggly candy worms had been dumped at the foot of her bed.

Sabrina and Salem exchanged a look.

"I have a feeling," Sabrina said, "that my troubles aren't over."

Chapter 4

☆

The next morning at school a very sleepy Sabrina spun her combination lock, clicked it open, then swung open her locker door.

An avalanche of Chinese fortune cookies tumbled out.

Just as Vice-Principal Kraft walked by.

Sabrina cringed.

But this time Mr. Kraft didn't say anything. He just scribbled something in his notebook. Then he said, "I don't care how nice your aunt is."

Unfortunately the halls weren't empty today. They were filled with students dashing to class.

"Now we know why Sabrina has that little weight problem," Libby joked as she and Mei, Jill, and Cee-Cee stepped around the pile of fortune cookies.

Titters rippled up and down the hall.

Sabrina felt a hand on her shoulder, and she turned to find Mark Wong. He wasn't laughing at her. "Need some help?" he said with a smile that suddenly made her feel a whole lot better.

Sabrina nodded. "I could use a hand."

Sabrina blinked another trash bag into her locker, then pulled it out and began to clean up with Mark's help.

"Fortune cookies," Mark said, shaking his head. "Why fortune cookies?"

"Why any of it?" Sabrina said with a shrug. She scooped up a handful of fortune cookies and stuffed them into the bag.

But when she reached toward the cookie pile again, she suddenly felt an uncontrollable urge. She couldn't help herself! She loved fortune cookies. She picked one at random, quickly cracked the crispy cookie in two, then pulled out the tiny paper fortune and read. "No kidding," she muttered with a wry smile.

"What does it say?" Mark asked.

"It says, 'Bad luck will be your shadow.' " Sabrina laughed. "Finally—a fortune cookie fortune that's really true!"

But Mark frowned.

"What's wrong?" Sabrina asked.

"Think about it," Mark said. "Fortune cookies usually have positive good-luck messages in them, like 'You will go on a long voyage' or 'find good fortune' or 'meet a tall, handsome stranger.' What restaurant would want to hand out bad fortunes to its customers? It's not good business."

Sabrina crumpled the fortune and popped it in the trash bag. "Maybe I should pick another one." She scanned the pile, searching for the cookie that would bring her good luck. At last she selected one, cracked it open, and read the fortune inside.

Sabrina gasped.

"What!" Mark asked.

"It's the same thing! 'Bad luck will be your shadow.'"

"No! You're kidding!" Mark took the slip from her hand and read it, then shook his head in disbelief. "That's weird."

Sabrina felt goose bumps tiptoe up her spine as she snatched up a third cookie and crushed it open. "Same fortune!"

Together, she and Mark cracked open a dozen fortune cookies.

Each one had exactly the same message.

"Bad luck will be your shadow."

Sabrina's eyes met Mark's. His dark brown eyes looked worried.

"Maybe someone got a special deal because these were reject fortunes?" Sabrina suggested. But the idea sounded lame even to her.

"I don't think this is a coincidence," Mark said. "I think somebody's trying to send you a message."

He looked so worried, Sabrina made herself smile. "Don't worry," she said. "It's probably just some big joke. I'll find out who it is soon."

* * *

Sabrina pushed through the door to the girls' room. *I need to find out who's doing this!* she told herself.

She went to the sink and turned on the cold water, then leaned over to splash her face. Behind her, she heard someone come into the room.

Sabrina straightened up, her eyes closed tight against the water, feeling for the paper towel holder. . . .

Someone handed her a towel. "Thanks," she said as she dried her face.

Then she opened her eyes. A dark-eyed face seemed to hover in the mirror like a ghost.

Sabrina gasped and whirled around.

Mei stood there staring at her with a puzzled look on her face. "Sabrina, are you okay?"

Sabrina laughed shakily and nodded. "I'm fine." She kept nodding, as if to reassure herself. "Not really."

"Can I do something to help you?" Mei asked.

Sabrina shook her head and tossed the paper towel into the overflowing trash bin. "No. Thanks. It's just . . ."

"What?" Mei prompted.

Sabrina glanced up at the girl. She really didn't want to admit it, but the girl did seem very nice. "It's just . . . somebody keeps playing these practical jokes on me."

Mei frowned slightly, tilting her head to one side. "What is 'practical joke'?" she asked. "Is it not fun to play them?"

Sabrina opened her mouth, then chuckled. She wasn't sure why they were called practical. "They're not like fun jokes told to make you laugh. They're pranks—you know, tricks a person plays on somebody else. They're usually harmless, but they can be mean, too. And they're not fun for the person who's the target. . . . Did that make any sense?"

Mei laughed. "Yes. I understand. We play such tricks at home, too. My little brother is the *worst!*"

Sabrina nodded. "One joke can be funny. Maybe even two. But someone is targeting me with them. And I can't figure out who."

Mei took out a carved wooden brush and began to stroke it through her long dark hair. "Did someone just play one?"

"Yeah. Someone keeps filling up my locker with things. Yesterday I got showered with popcorn."

Mei giggled, then covered her mouth. "Oh, I am so sorry. I know it is not funny. But . . . it is funny the way you say it. A popcorn shower!"

It did sound funny, Sabrina admitted to herself. *Could I be making more of this than I should?*

But the message in the fortune cookie wasn't funny. "Just now the same thing happened—only it was fortune cookies."

"Fortune cookies?" Mei asked.

Sabrina nodded. "With bad fortunes inside."

"Ah! This I have never heard of," Mei said.

"I know, that's what was so scary about it."

"Maybe you should ask Mark Wong," Mei said mysteriously.

"Huh? Why Mark?"

Mei's eyes shuttered. "Don't you know? His family owns a fortune-cookie factory in Chinatown."

"What?" Sabrina exclaimed. Then she peered at the girl. "How do you know that?"

Mei flipped her hair over her shoulder, then dropped her brush into her purse. "I saw him there—*we* saw him there. Libby and I. When I first came to Westbridge, Libby took me to Chinatown for dinner."

Hmm, Sabrina thought. *Strange that Mark didn't mention it when we were talking about fortune cookies in class yesterday.* She shrugged. Maybe it didn't seem unusual to him if it had always been the family business. "But Mark's my friend," Sabrina said. "Why would he pull pranks on me?"

Mei looked away again. "Oh, I am so sorry. I say the wrong thing. Mark . . ." And then she began to talk quickly in Chinese.

"Whoa, slow down!" Sabrina said.

Mei covered her mouth and laughed. "So sorry. Sometimes when I get nervous, I forget and talk in Chinese." She slipped her purse over her shoulder and picked up her books, then headed for the door.

"But wait," Sabrina said. "What were you saying about Mark?"

"Oh, he is a very nice boy, I'm sure." Mei smiled, then quick as a fox disappeared out the door.

Sabrina frowned. Mark did act nervous around her. And he'd been right there when the fortune cookies fell out of her locker. And his family made fortune cookies? How suspicious could you get?

But what about the popcorn? she asked herself. And the fruit punch over the door? And the black stuff on her microscope?

He did sit right next to her in science class. He could have blackened their microscope as easily as anyone, then acted nice to throw her off the track.

But why? It didn't make sense.

Sabrina spent the rest of the day walking around paranoid. Whenever she saw Harvey with Mei, she went the other way. She didn't feel like dealing with that whole problem now. She was too busy watching out for pranks.

After school Mark met her by her locker.

"Need a bodyguard?" Mark joked.

Sabrina grinned. "Maybe. Do you know a good one?"

Mark looked around, then held out his arms. "I'm free."

"You're hired," Sabrina joked back. "What do you suggest?"

Mark thought a moment. "Maybe what we should do is outwit whoever's doing it."

Sabrina closed her locker and swung her back-pack up onto her shoulder. "Like how?"

"Change your routine," Mark said. "Spend your afternoon with me."

Sabrina glanced down at her feet as they walked toward the exit. Was Mark flirting with her?

"Working on our project," Mark added quickly. He pushed open the front door. "Want to go to the library?"

"Well . . ." She glanced over her shoulder and saw Harvey and Mei walking their way.

"Sounds like a great idea," Sabrina said. "Come on, let's go."

Sabrina and Mark spent the entire afternoon at the library, doing research for their project. When Sabrina called home to let her aunts know where she was, she found out they were going to be out for the evening. So she and Mark stopped for a pizza at the Slicery on the way home.

"Looking for somebody?" Mark asked when they stepped in-side and waited for a table.

Sabrina hadn't realized she'd been that obvious. "No, just looking to see if any tables are about to empty." She had been looking for someone—Harvey and Mei. But they were nowhere in the crowd.

Forget about it, she told herself. *You're here with Mark. He's a good friend and lots of fun. Enjoy yourself.*

So she did. They had so much fun, it was growing dark by the time they left. When Mark walked her home, he lingered on the doorstep.

"Um, do you want to come in or something?" Sabrina asked, opening the door.

Mark hesitated. "Maybe next time. I gotta get home. Gotta feed my cat."

"You've got a cat?"

"Yeah. His name's Elvis. I named him that 'cause he can really wail."

Sabrina laughed. "My cat Salem's pretty good at that, too. I'd love to meet Elvis sometime."

"I'll see if I can arrange an appointment."

Just then Salem prowled out of the house, studying Mark with his glowing yellow eyes.

"Well, here he is now," Sabrina said, "my nice, ordinary house cat. Right, Salem?" She picked him up and hugged him to her cheek. "No talking!" she whispered.

Mark scratched Salem behind the ears. "Nice to meet you, Salem. Beautiful cat. American shorthair, right?"

"And darn proud of it," Sabrina said, nodding.

With a grin and a wave, Mark walked backward across the old Victorian home's painted wooden porch, then turned and jumped down over all the steps to the sidewalk. "See ya!" he called out, then disappeared into the night.

Cool guy, Sabrina thought as she shut the front door and hurried upstairs to her room.

Salem sat on the foot of her bed, eating a plate of

linguine with clam sauce her aunts had whipped up for him before they left for the evening. Sabrina zapped herself into a pair of pajamas, then slipped her feet into her slippers, and—

"Ewww!"

"What?" Salem said. "Do I have sauce on my chin?"

Sabrina kicked off her slippers. "No—there's something in my—*ewww!* What is it?"

Salem looked over the edge of the bed and sniffed. "Smells like banana pudding."

"In my slippers?"

"Don't look at me," Salem said. "I don't eat fruit in my current physical incarnation."

"It feels awful!" With a shiver, Sabrina pointed her finger and instantly made the pudding disappear.

"Now, that's what I call instant pudding," Salem quipped.

"I'll never eat banana pudding again," Sabrina said with a shudder. "I don't think I'll ever wear slippers again."

Sabrina excused herself to go to the bathroom and brush her teeth.

Salem slurped a strand of pasta into his mouth.

"AAAGGHHH!"

Salem nearly choked on his pasta. "Now what!"

Sabrina stormed back into her room, gritting her teeth. "Toothpaste on the toilet seat."

"That's a definite *ewww*," Salem replied.

Sabrina sighed. "Maybe this is some kind of weird magic. Maybe it's like a twenty-four-hour bug—and it'll be gone tomorrow." She brushed her hair a few strokes, then slid into bed.

Her feet only went down halfway.

"Short-sheeted your bed, huh?" Salem said. "I hate it when that happens."

Sabrina climbed out of bed and pulled off the sheet. "How long have you been here? Did you see anybody?"

"Not a soul," Salem said. "Mortal or magical."

"Well, one thing's for sure," Sabrina said.

"And that would be?"

"Now I know it's definitely not Mark. I've been with him since school got out. There's no way he could have sneaked in here and done all this. At least, not the mortal way."

"Absolutely," Salem said. "Unless."

"Unless what?"

"Unless he cut class and snuck over here to do it during school," Salem said.

"Surely you would have seen him!" Sabrina said.

"Maybe, maybe not," Salem said. "After all, I am but a simple mortal cat, a cat who sleeps pretty soundly after lunch."

Sabrina picked a new paperback off her shelf, then slipped into bed to read herself to sleep. "I still can't believe Mark would do these mean tricks," she said, lying back against her pillow.

Crunch!

"Excuse me," Salem said. "But did your pillow just say, 'Crunch'?"

Sabrina sat up and looked inside her pillow. "Cap'n Crunch cereal!"

"Ooh, can I have some?" Salem asked. "It satisfies my feline desire for kibble but with so much more fun."

Sabrina threw her pillow at him. "You can have it all!" Then she zapped herself a new pillow and laid back to read.

Tomorrow, she told herself, *I'm definitely going to find out who's doing this!*

Chapter 5

The next morning at school Sabrina barely blinked as an avalanche of soapsuds cascaded from her opened locker.

Of course, Mr. Kraft was there. He'd made her locker a regular stop on his morning route just to see what would tumble out next.

"At least it'll be easy to clean up!" she quipped to the vice principal.

He didn't crack a smile.

"Is *this* your science experiment?" Harvey asked as he and Valerie walked up to her.

"Nope, just doing my laundry."

"Really?" Harvey asked. "In your locker?"

"Harvey, I was just kidding!"

"Oh. Yeah." He chuckled. "I knew that. Oh, Sabrina, I wanted to ask you—"

"Harvey . . ."

Harvey stopped when he heard Mei's voice. "Hi, Mei. Hi, Libby."

Libby stared at the soap bubbles covering the floor. "These cries for attention are so pitiful, Sabrina."

Magic jumped in Sabrina's finger, but she squelched the desire to turn Libby into a mop to clean it up.

By the time she looked back at Harvey, Mei had taken hold of him and was leading him away. "Can you help me, Harvey? My locker's stuck."

"Bye, Harvey," Sabrina said, but he didn't even hear her.

"Looks like Harvey's getting too smart to hang out with a freak like you anymore," Libby said before following them.

Sabrina shook her head as she watched them walk away. "Just look at them," Sabrina said to Valerie. "She says come and Harvey just follows."

"Sabrina, I'm shocked at you!" Valerie exclaimed.

"What?"

"That's how wars get started!"

"But I—"

"Besides," Valerie went on, "it's not a nice way to behave toward a visitor to our country."

"But . . . but she's stealing my boyfriend!" Sabrina sputtered.

"Well, maybe you need to learn to share with foreign visitors," Valerie suggested.

Sabrina shook her head. This was outrageous. Did Mei have *everyone* totally snowed? So she was nice. *Big deal! I'm nice, too!* she wanted to shout. *At least, I am when beautiful girls aren't trying to steal my boyfriend!*

Ha, trying? Succeeding is more like it!

"Besides, Mei is sweet," Valerie went on. "She and Libby invited me over for a sleepover Friday night."

"What!"

Valerie acted hurt. "Don't act so surprised, Sabrina. Maybe you're not the only one who thinks I can be a good friend."

"Oh, Val, don't go!" Sabrina said. "Libby must be up to something."

"What, you don't think I'm good enough to get invited to Libby's house?"

"No, I just think it's a little odd that—"

"You're just jealous," Val said.

"Jealous?"

"Yeah, you're trying to keep me from having popular friends!" She turned and stomped off toward her first class.

"Val, wait—"

But Valerie didn't even turn around. *This is nuts,* Sabrina thought as she kicked at some of the bubbles. *Has everyone fallen under Mei's spell?*

"Hey, Sabrina, wait!" Mark shoved through the crowded hall to catch up with her.

"Hey, Mark. What's the matter?"

"I have something for you," he said. He held out his hand. A small rounded basket dangled from a leather strap.

Sabrina brightened. She was feeling kind of sorry for herself. At least somebody cared. "For me?" she asked. "What is it?"

"Open it," he said.

Sabrina lifted the lid off—and nearly dropped it.

"Is this another prank?" Sabrina exclaimed.

Inside the tiny basket was a bug!

"No!" Mark cried. He reached out and caught the tiny basket just as Sabrina was about to drop it. "How could you think that? It's a present. From me . . . and my grandmother."

"Your grandmother gives bugs for presents?" Sabrina asked.

"It's not just a bug—it's a cricket," Mark explained.

Sabrina looked at the bug, waving it's long hair-like feelers at her.

"Crickets are good luck." Mark shrugged. "I mean, it's not like I *really* believe all this stuff. But I told my grandmother about your bad luck, and she insisted I bring it. I figure it couldn't hurt. Maybe it will guard you against some of the pranks."

Sabrina relaxed and eyed the little bug. Maybe he wasn't so bad after all. And she'd certainly more remarkable things in her life than a good-luck cricket. "Thanks, Mark. I can use all the good luck I can get." She grinned and gave Mark a quick friendly hug. "And thank your grandmother for me, too."

Mark hugged her back.

"Um, Mark. You can let go now."

"Uh, yeah." Mark blushed and ran his hand through his thick black hair. "Well, gotta go."

"That's what I was going to say," she said as she watched him dash off to class.

Feeling a little better, Sabrina headed off to math class.

She sat down in her chair and pulled out her book, notebook, and pencils.

"Sabrina," Mrs. Quick called. "Would you please come to the board and show us how you worked Problem 1?"

Inwardly Sabrina groaned. She was pretty good at math—probably thanks to some genes she shared with Aunt Zelda. But she hated going up to the board to work problems.

Oh, well. Gotta go, I guess.

She tried to get up—but found she couldn't.

She felt stuck—stuck to her chair.

Sabrina struggled. Was this another prank? Or some kind of weird magic.

"Sabrina, we're waiting." Mrs. Quick held up the chalk expectantly.

With one mighty effort Sabrina ripped herself from her chair—literally.

"Oops." Sabrina was up. But the back of her skirt was still down. She stared at her chair. It was obvious now what had happened. Someone had put glue on her chair!

All around her kids began to giggle and snicker. It was totally embarrassing!

Mrs. Quick looked startled. "Sabrina! What is it, dear?"

"I . . . I think someone put some kind of glue on my chair!"

With that the classroom burst into laughter.

Mrs. Quick looked totally startled.

But Mei sat near the front of the room, and she jumped up to grab Mrs. Quick's overcoat from a hook by the door. Then she hurried over to wrap the coat around Sabrina's shoulders.

"Thanks," Sabrina whispered.

"All right, class, that's enough!" Mrs. Quick called out. Then she turned back to Sabrina. "Would you like to go to the office, dear? Is there anyone you can call to bring you some new clothes?"

"Yeah, I'd like to do that. Thanks, Mrs. Quick."

As Sabrina headed out the door, she heard Mrs. Quick say, "All right, then. I want to know right now who's responsible for this silly prank."

Sabrina had a feeling she wouldn't find out.

Once out in the hall, Sabrina dashed for the nearest girls' room. After checking that no one else was inside, she quickly zapped her torn skirt into a pair of jeans. She felt like conjuring up a suit of armor, but she had doubts that even that would help.

"This is getting really annoying!" Sabrina mumbled. When she walked back into the hall, she spotted Mark pushing some audiovisual equipment to the office.

"Mark," she said, catching him by the shoulder.

Mark's eyes lit up when he saw her. "Sabrina, hi. How's your day been?"

"Terrible." She told him about the latest prank.

Mark's eyes clouded over, and he took Sabrina's hands in his. "Sabrina, I don't like this. I'm getting worried."

"Me, too," Sabrina said.

Mark looked as if he were debating something in his mind. At last he said, "I want you to come with me this afternoon."

Sabrina swallowed. "Where?"

"Promise you won't laugh?"

"Promise."

"To see my grandmother."

Sabrina looked puzzled. "Why would that make me laugh?"

"Well, let's just say she knows about things," Mark said. "Maybe she can help you."

"But what do you mean?" Sabrina began.

But before Mark could answer, Mr. Kraft spotted them from down the hall. "Quick! Get back to class," Mark told her. "I've got a legitimate reason for being out here. I'll stall him."

"Thanks."

"I'll meet you at your locker after school!" he called after her.

Sabrina didn't know what a visit with Mark's grandmother might do to help, but she was ready to try anything.

Mark's grandmother lived in an old house not far from the school. The porch overflowed with all kinds of flowering plants and herbs, many Sabrina had never seen before. Inside, her home was warm and inviting, decorated with many pieces of furniture and objects from her homeland. A black-and-white cat wandered silently into the entryway and rubbed up against Sabrina's leg.

"Come here, Elvis," Mark said as he scooped up the cat.

"Is that your cat?" Sabrina asked. "He's really gorgeous. Do you live here? With your grandmother?"

"What? Oh, the cat. No. I live with my folks in Oakcliff. But we didn't know till after I got Elvis that my dad's horribly allergic to cats. But I was too attached to him by the time we found out. I couldn't give him up. So grandmother lets me keep him here. Come on," he said, leading her into the living room. "Sit down." Sabrina sat down in a comfortable overstuffed rocking chair.

"Grandmother!" Mark called down the hall. "We're here!"

Sabrina stood up as Mark's grandmother came into the room carrying a tray with a teapot and cups. She was shorter than Sabrina, but walked with a regal air. Her smile was warm and genuine. "Sabrina," she said with a strong Asian accent, "it is so nice to meet you. Mark speaks well of you."

"Thank you," Sabrina said, pretending not to notice Mark's blush. "You have a lovely home here."

"Thank you." She set the tray down on the black lacquered coffee table and stood up to look around. "It is filled with good memories, and that makes it a wonderful place to be. But please, sit." She poured them all some green tea, then sat back with the steaming cup held between both hands. "Now, tell me what troubles you."

"I told her a little bit about the pranks," Mark explained.

Sabrina took a sip of the delicious tea, then began to tell Grandmother Chu about the pranks, one by one. "Most of the pranks sound kind of silly, I know," Sabrina said.

"Not at all," Grandmother Chu replied. "Something that troubles you is never silly. Tell me. Have you seen any unusual animals?"

Sabrina exchanged a look with Mark. Salem's pretty unusual, she thought with a grin. But of course, she didn't mention him. "Not really. . . ."

Grandmother Chu bit her lower lip and rocked a little in her chair. "There is a legend in my country," she said. "Many pooh-pooh it today as superstition. The legend is of the fox, a magical fox, that can live for hundreds of years. Some say a thousand. The fox is a trickster who loves more than anything to torment good people. This fox," she said, leaning forward, "can transform itself into human shape."

Sabrina shot a look at Mark. He was shifting uneasily in his chair.

"Sometimes it appears as an old man," Grandmother Chu went on. "But it is when the fox appears as a pretty young girl that it does most of its mischief."

Tiny prickles danced down Sabrina's spine. Mei was from China. And if Harvey's reaction to her was any indication, she was certainly a fox.

Could she be . . . ?

No, it couldn't be. It's just too awful a pun!

Could her prankster not be a kid at all, but a foreign exchange student who was really a Chinese fox? A magical being from another realm?

Suddenly there was a knock at the door.

Mark jumped up from his chair. "I'll get it, Grandmother."

Grandmother Chu leaned forward and took Sabrina by the hand, her black eyes full of sincerity. "Mark, he is more American than Chinese. He tries to throw off the old thoughts and ideas and thinks only of science and technology, like his computer games and web sites. He seems to have forgotten all the stories I told him as a child, and he ignores the magic in the world. But you and I—" she chuckled softly—"we see the magic, eh?"

Sabrina nodded, wondering if the old woman sensed something about her own magic.

But before they could talk more, Mark came back in, with a surprise visitor.

"Aunt Zelda, what are you doing here?" Sabrina asked. "How did you know I was here?"

"That's not important right now." She turned and smiled at Grandmother Chu and greeted her in Chinese.

The old woman smiled in delight and answered back in Chinese.

"Hey, your aunt speaks Chinese better than I do!" Mark whispered.

"Yeah, she's studied a lot of languages over the years." Sabrina didn't say how many years. "It's sort of a hobby."

But then Zelda's eyes took on a worried look as she pulled Sabrina to the side. "Sabrina, it's urgent, you have to come home right away!"

Chapter 6

☆

hy? What's wrong?" Sabrina searched her
aunt's face for clues.

"I . . ." She glanced at Mark and his grandmother.
"I'll tell you when we get home. Now hurry . . ."

Sabrina grabbed her backpack and sweater.
"Thank you for the tea," she told Mark's grandmother.

Mark walked Sabrina and Zelda to the door.
"Anything I can do?" he asked quietly.

Sabrina just smiled and shook her head.

"I'll call you later tonight," Mark promised.

Sabrina smiled, then left with her aunt.

Once outside, Sabrina grabbed Aunt Zelda's arm.
"Aunt Zelda, what's wrong?"

Aunt Zelda looked both ways, then led Sabrina into
the shadows. "Shall we go?" The two witches snapped
their fingers, and seconds later found themselves back
on the front porch of the Spellmans' Victorian home.

Sabrina yanked open the door and held it for her aunt.

But Aunt Zelda shook her head. "You go on in, Sabrina. I . . . I'll be in in a minute."

"What? But—"

"Just go!" Aunt Zelda shoved her across the threshold, then pulled the door closed.

Totally confused, Sabrina looked around. She spotted Aunt Hilda sitting on the couch drinking lemonade and arguing with the TV.

"Francesca—are you crazy?" Hilda shouted at an actress with big hair on a daytime soap. "Don't listen to Roger! He's two-timing you behind your back with your half-sister from your mother's third marriage! While you're working third shift at the hospital!"

"Yeah, Earth to Francesca," Salem cat-called from his perch on the back of the couch. "You can't trust Roger. He hates your cat—so what part of this do you *not* understand?"

"Aunt Hilda! Salem!" Sabrina exclaimed. "How can you watch soaps at a time like this?"

Hilda looked over her shoulder at her niece, glanced at her watch, then frowned. "At a time like what? It's four twenty-five."

Sabrina strode over, flicked off the TV with a dash of magic sparkles, then turned to glare at them. "At a time like . . . you know. Whatever it is that's wrong." Sabrina paused a moment. "And, by the way, what *is* wrong?"

"Nothing's wrong," Salem complained, "except that you made us miss the last five minutes of *As the World Churns*. Now we'll have to wait till tomorrow to find out whether Francesca lets that slimy Roger make a fool of her—again."

"I can't believe how heartless you two are!" Sabrina exclaimed. "What about Aunt Zelda?"

"What about me, dear?" Aunt Zelda asked cheerfully as she glided down the stairs wearing lavender exercise clothes and daintily dabbing at her perspiring brow.

Sabrina rushed to meet her aunt at the foot of the stairs. "Aunt Zelda, are you all right? And—" Sabrina frowned. "What are you doing inside? I just left you on the front porch!"

"No, you didn't, dear."

"Yes, I *did*."

"No, you did not, young lady. I've been up in my room doing yoga and tai chi for the past hour."

"But . . . but . . ." Sabrina looked back and forth between her two aunts, "What about the emergency?"

Zelda exchanged a glance with Hilda. "What emergency, dear?"

"Grrr! The one you told me about!"

"When?"

"When you came to get me at Mark's grandmother's house!"

Aunt Zelda stood there with her mouth hanging

open, staring at Sabrina as if she'd suddenly started speaking the one Chinese dialect that she wasn't fluent in. Without a word she took Sabrina by the arm and gently led her over to the couch to sit down between her and Aunt Hilda.

"Now, Sabrina, dear, just sit here and take a nice deep breath. In through your nose—one, two, three, four. . . . Out through your mouth more slowly—one, two, three, four, five, six. . . . Again, in . . ."

Sabrina knew it was hopeless to argue with her persistent aunt, so she humored her and breathed in and out a few quick times.

"Sabrina, dear, the idea is to relax—not hyperventilate," her aunt commented.

"But how can I?" Sabrina exclaimed, "when something awful has happened."

Aunt Zelda exchanged a worried glance with Hilda, then said, "I'm not sure what's got you so excited, but I've been here all afternoon."

"No, you haven't."

"Yes, I have—"

"No, you—"

"Don't start that again," Hilda interrupted, putting her hands up between the two witches. "Sabrina, Zelda and I have both been here, in the house, all afternoon. I promise."

"And I'm a witness," Salem put in, then muttered, "I haven't been able to sneak a can of tuna or even a goldfish cracker since lunchtime."

"But then who—?" Sabrina jumped up from the

couch and ran to the front door. She yanked it open and ran out onto the porch.

"You're not here!" Sabrina exclaimed.

"Of course not, dear," Aunt Zelda called politely from her graceful perch on the couch. "I'm over here."

"Oh, dear," Hilda said to her sister. "I hope she's not coming down with some strange mortal virus."

"I'm *not* sick," Sabrina insisted. "I'm just—" She broke off when she saw the tail of a fox disappearing through the shrubbery across the street.

"Ohmygosh. The fox. The Chinese fox. The one Grandmother Chu told me about!" She came back inside and sat down on the couch, then quickly told her aunts what Grandmother Chu had told her.

Aunt Zelda shook her head. "I have known a Chinese fox or two in my life. They are quite mischievous."

"I'm going over to Libby's right now," Sabrina said. "Somehow I've got to find out if Mei might be this magical fox Mark's grandmother told me about.

"Wait, Sabrina," Aunt Zelda said. "I have something that might help." With a snap of her fingers a small gilded hand mirror appeared in her lap. She picked it up and smiled as she patted a stray wisp of hair back from her forehead.

"A mirror?" Sabrina asked, taking it from her aunt. She peered at herself in the mirror—a perfect image of herself stared back. "How will a plain old mirror help?" she asked.

"Ah, this is no ordinary mirror," Zelda explained. "It's kind of like the one that Snow White's wicked stepmother had—remember?"

Sabrina nodded.

"Although this one works a little differently. Hilda got me this portable model during the Middle Ages when I was dating a handsome ogre . . ." She sighed wistfully, ". . . who just happened to be concealing the fact that he had two heads—not that I'm prejudiced, mind you. I just prefer a man who's honest in his relationships."

Hilda nodded. "Boy, do I remember that guy!" She leaned toward Sabrina. "I tried to tell Zelda for *weeks* that Jean-Paul was two-faced—he didn't have two names for nothing! But she was too much in love to listen. She had to see it for herself."

"So . . . I don't get it," Sabrina said. "How did this mirror help?"

Zelda smiled at her favorite niece. "The True You mirror is special—one look and it reveals who you *really* are. Now, *you* see an unchanged image of yourself for a very special reason, because you are always yourself. At least, most of the time," she added, thinking of a few times Sabrina had disguised herself. "A very admirable trait, by the way."

"Thanks."

"But now try holding the True You mirror up in front of Salem," Zelda suggested.

Before Sabrina could move, the sleek black cat yowled and dashed behind the living room drapes.

"Salem! Come back here!" Zelda called.

"Heh-heh, no offense, Zelda," the cat said without coming out, "but isn't there some superstition about black cats and mirrors?"

"You're mixing things up," Zelda said with a laugh, "and besides, you know those old superstitions aren't true."

"But . . . but maybe," Salem whimpered, "the real me is . . . revo-o-olting!"

Zelda laughed and knelt to pull the curtains away. "Don't worry, Salem," she said, stroking the sobbing cat's fur. "True, you can be quite a sneak when you want to be—"

"I can't help it—it's what cats do!" Salem whined.

"But nothing bad is going to happen. Come on, trust me. Let Sabrina see you in the mirror."

"Oh, all right," Salem whined. "But don't blame me if you don't like what you see!"

Salem leaped onto the back of the couch.

Sabrina started to hold up the mirror—

"Wait!" Salem exclaimed. He licked his front right paw, then groomed the fur on his face and head. "Okay, ready."

Sabrina giggled, then held up the mirror.

Purring, Salem preened this way and that. "My, my, my, what a handsome ca—Hey! Wait a minute! That's *me!*"

Zelda grinned. "I know it's you."

"But I mean, me—Salem Saberhagen! Not the

devilishly handsome black American shorthair, but Salem Saberhagen, the devilishly handsome dark-haired warlock!"

Sabrina's eyes widened in surprise. Instead of reflecting the black cat face that the Witches' Council had sentenced Salem to endure for a hundred years, the True You mirror reflected the true Salem, the human—or rather, superhuman—face he'd been born with.

"Because that's the true you!" Sabrina exclaimed happily.

"Either way, I'm rather debonair, don't you think?" Salem purred, turning this way and that to admire himself . . .

Sabrina hugged the black cat. "You're all that." She hugged Aunt Zelda, too. "And you're terrific. This will be perfect! If I can get Mei to look in the True You mirror, I'll be able to tell for sure if she's really a Chinese exchange student—or a Chinese fox!"

Sabrina took the shortcut, that is, the witch express, to the street where Libby Chessler lived. Her house was easy to find—not just because it was the biggest house on the block, but because it was the showiest. Sabrina hurried past the fountain, hurried up the many winding steps that led to the huge French doors. She rang the doorbell—and the first lines of Beethoven's Fifth Symphony rang through the house.

Sabrina rolled her eyes and waited for someone to come to the door.

A flick of the elegant curtains at the window nearest the door told Sabrina that someone had peeked out. She waited a few minutes; when still no one answered the door, she rang the doorbell again.

At last the door opened a little, and Libby poked her head out. She gave Sabrina's outfit a quick condescending once-over, then quipped, "Sorry—we already bought Girl Scout cookies from the little girl next door." She started to slam the door, but Sabrina pretended to cough to cover a whispered:

Chessler door,
Stick to the floor.

"Hey!" Libby complained, tugging on the doorknob. "What's wrong with this stupid door?"

"I guess it's stuck," Sabrina said and used the gap to slip inside.

"Hey, you can't just come in here—I didn't invite you!"

"I'm not here to see you," Sabrina replied. "I'm here to see Mei."

"Well, you can't see her, either," Libby insisted, jumping in front of Sabrina. "We're busy . . . organizing accessories."

"Oh, gosh, I hate to interrupt that," Sabrina said sarcastically as she squeezed past. "But I'm afraid this is important. Besides, shouldn't Mei decide for herself if she wants to see me?"

Libby sputtered and started to follow her—

"Uh, don't you think you ought to shut the door?" Sabrina suggested as she secretly flicked her finger over her shoulder and whispered,

In swarms a surprise—
Big black flies!

Then she added more loudly, so Libby could hear: "You don't want to let in flies, do you?"

Libby whirled back toward the door.

A swarm of huge black flies buzzed just over the doorjamb.

"Ewww!" Libby hurried back to struggle with the door, swatting around her hair as she ran.

That should keep her busy, at least for a few minutes, Sabrina thought as she strode down the polished marble hallway to Libby's room. She'd been in Libby's house a couple of times before, but she still almost felt as if she needed a road map to find her way through the cavernous mansion.

When she arrived at Libby's open doorway, Mei jumped to her feet as if startled, scattering necklaces, belts, and scarves across the floor.

Whoa—so they were REALLY sorting accessories? Sabrina thought, shaking her head. *That is so sick. . . .*

"Why, Sabrina," Mei said, recovering instantly to

73

give Sabrina a friendly smile. "Hello. It is good to see you."

"Oh, *really?*" Sabrina asked.

"Why, of course," Mei said, sitting down on the bed again. "It is always good to see a good friend."

"That sounds like a fortune-cookie fortune to me," Sabrina said.

Mei giggled her laughing-brook laugh. "Maybe you should just call me Cookie."

Sabrina looked around, trying to think of a casual way to get Mei's ruby earrings on the floor. "Oh, my. Look at these!" she exclaimed, scooping them up. "Why, they would look just awesome on you, Mei."

"Really?" Mei's eyes lit up, and she reached for the jewels.

Appeals to your foxy vanity, hmm? Sabrina thought. As the girl put on the earrings, Sabrina slipped the True You mirror out of her bag. Then she sat down on the bed beside Mei, so she could see clearly what Mei's face would look like in the mirror.

"Here," Sabrina said. "Look."

Mei eagerly reached for the mirror to admire herself. Sabrina held it up for her but wouldn't let go.

This is it—this is the moment, Sabrina thought. She peered into the mirror, too, as Mei gazed into the magical glass.

A face smiled back—but it was not the face of a dark-haired girl.

It was the hairy face of a dark brown fox!

Beneath it's pointy brown ears, it's eyes were the same dark brown as Mei's, It's dark red tongue hung out between huge pointed teeth.

Mei's smile—the one on her beautiful young human girl face—froze. For a moment she was as still as if she'd stopped breathing.

Then she screamed—an eerie high-pitched *Scream*-worthy scream—

Crack!

That shattered the mirror into a spiderweb of cracks.

But it didn't matter. The magic had worked. Sabrina had seen the truth in the True You mirror.

Mei was a Chinese fox!

"Gotcha!" Sabrina whispered.

Mei jumped to her feet and shot Sabrina the strangest half grin, half glare she'd ever seen.

A second later she shimmered like heat waves on hot asphalt—and the beautiful young girl transformed into a sleek brown fox.

Sabrina's heart lurched. Her witch half had many magical powers at her fingertips, but her human half couldn't help but experience a moment of terror as she stared into the fox's slobbery jaws.

She'd read *Little Red Riding Hood* at a *very* young age.

Okay, so that was actually not a fox, but a wolf, Sabrina thought. *Close enough when the teeth are inches from your nose.*

But the fox didn't lunge or snap off Sabrina's nose. It did something far stranger.

It bent its front leg and dipped its head—almost in a bow of acknowledgment.

Then, before Sabrina could speak, it turned and leaped through Libby's window into the backyard.

A neat trick, since the window wasn't open.

Sabrina shook her head in amazement. She ran to the window and looked out.

The fox had disappeared.

Chapter 7

Gotta go!

Sabrina stepped to the center of the room. *Gotta find out why that fox is pestering me—so I can make it stop!*

First she stuffed the broken True You mirror into her backpack. She hoped it wouldn't bring her bad luck, like the time she broke a talking mirror and had a whole week's worth of bad luck.

But then, she hadn't actually broken this mirror. Mei's unreal scream had.

Sabrina raised her hand above her head, preparing to transport herself magically into the backyard, when—

Libby stormed into the room. "What are you doing, *freak?*" she shouted. "I told you not to come in here. Did you touch anything?" She looked around the room, then blanched. "Where's Mei?" she demanded.

Sabrina shrugged. "She, uh . . . had to run."

"What?" Libby exclaimed. "Run where?"

"I wish I knew," Sabrina answered truthfully.

"But she wouldn't," Libby insisted angrily. "Not without telling me. After we finished with the accessories, we were going to alphabetize my shoes!"

Don't touch that one, Sabrina told herself. With Libby here, she'd have to exit the mortal way, through the door, and she had to hurry if she wanted to catch that fox!

"But wait!" Libby demanded as Sabrina slipped around her and strode into the hallway. "What about Mei? If you said anything to make her leave—"

"I promise—it wasn't anything I *said,*" Sabrina replied, then and dashed out the door, through the maze of hallways, and out the front door into the yard.

It was growing dark outside, which would make it much harder to trail a dark-haired animal. She ran around to the side of the house toward the backyard, but a high fence blocked her path—and then a motion-activated security floodlight flashed on, temporarily blinding her with its strong light.

But it didn't really matter. The fox had a good ten- or fifteen-minute lead on her. It would be long gone by now.

Where was it headed? And how could she ever find it?

She tried a quick-tracer spell. She'd never done one on her own, but she'd seen her aunts do it. She checked her clothing. Yes! She plucked one tiny fox hair from her shirt. It was all she would need.

She placed the hair in the palm of her hand and above it made a secret hand motion with the other. She hoped she remembered it right.

Za-a-a-a-p!

Oops! I guess I should have asked permission, Sabrina thought.

She had just landed in Chinatown—in New York City! The sidewalks were crowded with residents and tourists, milling in and out of the many Chinese restaurants and shops. Delicious smells filled Sabrina's nostrils and her stomach growled, reminding her that she'd missed supper.

I'd better phone home, she thought and started to zap up a cell phone to call her aunts. *Then maybe I could just grab an egg roll or a pan-fried dumpling or two before I . . .*

A wisp of a fox tail at the end of the block caught her eye.

Dinner would have to wait. She had a fox to capture!

Sabrina started to run, then looked down at her feet. She loved her stacked black shoes, but they were definitely not designed for serious track work on city sidewalks. She ducked into a dark alley and chanted:

Lose the shoes
designed for show—
Show me some shoes
designed to go!

Sabrina felt a brief jolt shoot through her feet and looked down to find her tootsies encased in a sleek pair of sparkling white sneakers. So they weren't name brands—they looked just as good. Then she took off at a race-walk pace, trying not to attract attention as she hurried through the streets.

She rounded the corner—there! Dashing into that tiny shop. Sabrina hurried in, but found it deserted. Back on the street, she spotted the fox's tail again through the crowds and weaved herself through, turning this way and that.

Sabrina paused at the corner under a streetlight, confused. Which way now?

Then she felt someone tug on her sleeve. When she looked around, she saw an old woman looking up at her with a mysterious smile. The golden threads in her jacket sparkled under the bright streetlight. She said nothing, just pointed toward a small narrow alleyway.

"Did you see . . ." Sabrina paused, wondering if she'd sound crazy. "Did you see . . . a fox?"

The old woman just cackled and nodded, jabbing her finger again toward the alley.

Does she know . . . ? Sabrina wondered.

Did she see . . . ?

When Sabrina hesitated, the old woman gave her a gentle push toward the alley, smiling and nodding, but still not saying a word.

Sabrina nodded and followed the woman's directions. Maybe she, like Mark's grandmother, was more open to the magical elements in the universe and so saw things that other, more cynical people did not.

A movement at the entry to the alleyway made Sabrina quicken her pace. She dashed down the dark alley, her vision hindered at first as her pupils struggled to adjust to the dark.

Suddenly she screeched to a halt.

The alley abruptly dead-ended in a brick wall. There was no other way out. Cautiously Sabrina looked around, listening for a sound, perhaps of the fox hiding behind one of the trash cans or empty crates that lined the alley.

Nothing. Growing braver, she even kicked a few crates aside, searching for the mischievous creature, but she saw nothing. The alleyway was empty, except for her.

Sighing, she turned around to head back to the street—

And gasped!

A ten-foot wall of fire suddenly erupted across the width of the alley.

☆

Chapter 8

☆

You're a witch— Sabrina reminded herself as she eyed the fire. *Don't panic. You can get out of this with a flick of a forefinger.*

But the human side of her couldn't help but react with fear to the crackling leaping flames.

"I hope you brought the marshmallows," said someone behind her.

Someone who sounded an awful lot like a smart-aleck black cat!

Sabrina yanked her backpack from her shoulders and dropped it on the ground. A small furry head poked out.

"Salem! What are you doing here?"

"Perspiring?" Salem replied. Then his yellow eyes widened as he stared at how high the flames were now spreading

"You've got to stop sneaking along with me without being invited!" Sabrina yelled at the cat.

"It's unnerving. And dangerous, and really, really rude, especially when—"

"Uh, hate to interrupt, Sab, but . . . isn't it about time for you to say 'Gotta go!'—and hopefully take me with you? Pleasepleaseplease?"

"Oh, yeah." Sabrina picked up her cat-filled backpack and slung it back over her shoulder, then turned toward the fire. She had just raised her finger and begun to chant a spell to get them out of there when . . .

She stopped and stared. "Salem . . . did you notice something odd about this particular fire?"

"No, I didn't, and I don't care, just—"

Sabrina stepped toward the center of the flames.

"Are you crazy?" Salem yelped. "Uh, I've never mentioned this before, Sabrina, but I have a *very* strong aversion to being *burned alive!*"

"Me, too," Sabrina said. "But I don't think we need to worry about that." She raised her hand toward the crackling flames—

"Stop!" Salem shrieked.

But Sabrina didn't stop. She stuck her whole arm into the flames!

And nothing happened. She didn't burn herself. Not even when she, with a screaming Salem on her back, walked *through* the towering wall of fire.

"Look, Salem," she told her cat. "The flames aren't even hot!"

"But . . . but . . ." For once the chatty cat was speechless.

"It's an illusion," Sabrina explained, turning back to admire the vision. "An illusion of magic."

Salem nearly burst into tears with relief. "M-m-my fur . . . it's not even singed! But how . . . ?"

"The fox," Sabrina said. "Just another prank."

"Ha, ha," Salem complained.

"Yeah," Sabrina agreed. "Not very funny. Like most pranks."

And then, before their astonished eyes, the fire disappeared as quickly as it had appeared. Nothing remained—not a cinder, not a wisp of smoke—to show that the fire had ever been there at all.

"You know what that means," Sabrina said.

Salem licked his lips. "We can go eat Chinese now?"

"No," Sabrina said. "The fox must be nearby. It saw me walk through the fire. Once it realized I wasn't fooled, the fox made the fire disappear."

"No egg roll?" Salem whined.

"Not now," Sabrina said, heading toward the street. "Not when we have a fox to catch up with. Come on!"

"Do I have a choice?" Salem muttered as he ducked back down into Sabrina's backpack.

Back on the streets, Sabrina looked for a clue.

She didn't have to wait for long.

"Sabrina!" someone called.

Sabrina looked around.

"Up here!"

Sabrina looked up.

A girl with long dark hair waved at her from a second floor window.

"Mei!" Sabrina exclaimed.

"Come on up!" Mei called down to her. "Second floor. First door on right!"

"What's she up to?" Salem whispered.

"I don't know," Sabrina answered. "But I'm ready to find out." She opened the door to the building and took the stairs two at a time up the dark narrow stairwell.

When she reached the third-floor landing, she hesitated. Who knew what Mei or the fox (or whoever or whatever she was!) had planned for her. Was it a trap of some kind?

But these pranks have got to end, Sabrina told herself. So she put her hand on the doorknob and pushed open the door.

Inside she found a small neat living room, and beyond that—

"Oh, wow," Sabrina whispered. Beyond the living room was a dining table draped in a white tablecloth set for two. Candles flickered on the table and around the room.

"Finally," Salem exclaimed. "Dinner!" He leaped from Sabrina's backpack, then jumped up onto one of the chairs, his tail flicking as he drooled in anticipation. "I hope I can get sweet and sour shrimp!"

Sabrina frowned and looked around. "I just hope I can get some answers."

She jumped when the doorknob on a door to another room turned, and she braced herself for a showdown with Mei.

But it wasn't Mei who walked through the door.

Sabrina couldn't believe who it was!

"You!" she exclaimed in disbelief.

Chapter 9

☆

Mark Wong smiled at Sabrina as he came into the room carrying a huge tray of steaming Chinese food.

Sabrina took a step backward as her heart sank. What was Mark doing here? Was he somehow involved in these pranks after all? She was in total shock.

"Mark! What are you doing here?" Sabrina exclaimed. How could Mark possibly be in New York!

"Sabrina, please—sit down," Mark said as he slid the steaming dishes to the table. "I've ordered dinner for the two of us."

"But, Mark—what's going on? How'd you get here? Why are you here?" She nervously looked around the room. "Where's Mei?"

Mark frowned. "Mei? What about her?"

"Where is she?"

"How should I know?" He looked puzzled.

Was he? Or was he hiding something?

Then Sabrina had a strange thought. "Mark—how did you know I would be here?"

Mark just laughed. "Radar? Come on, Sabrina, sit down. Let's eat. Then we can talk." His eyes shone as if they held a great secret.

"But—"

"I've got pan-fried dumplings," he said with a teasing smile.

Sabrina dropped her backpack as Mark took her by the hand and led her to the table. His smile was so warm, and the food smelled so delicious, and Sabrina was so tired—tired of chasing an elusive fox . . .

"Well, maybe I could eat just a bite," she said gratefully.

Mark held out her chair as Sabrina sat down and put the white linen napkin in her lap.

"Great." Mark went around to the other side, but frowned when he saw Salem sitting there. "Hey, scram, you mangy cat!" And with that he shoved Salem out of the chair onto the floor and sat down in the chair himself. Then he placed his napkin in his lap as if nothing unusual had happened at all.

Uh-oh, don't blow your cover! Sabrina thought as she leaned down and snapped her fingers for Salem to come to her.

"How rude!" Salem whispered as he curled up beside her chair. "Why, if I had my powers, I'd—"

"Shhh!" Sabrina whispered back. "Behave yourself and I'll slip you an egg roll."

"Fine," Salem huffed, "but if I were you, I Wouldn't trust a guy who hates cats."

Sabrina frowned. Something about that comment bothered her, but before she could think about it, Mark leaned down on his side of the table. "Is everything all right, Sabrina?"

"I uh" —Sabrina dropped her chopsticks— "dropped my chopsticks!" She scooped them back up, then sat up and grinned, a little embarrassed and hoping he hadn't actually seen her talking to a cat.

Sabrina speared a dumpling and was about to stuff it into her mouth when—

"Wait!" Mark cried, holding out his hand.

"What?" Sabrina dropped her dumpling onto her plate and stared at it. "Is there something wrong with my dumpling?"

Mark laughed. "I just meant wait . . . we have to read our fortune cookies."

Sabrina looked at him in astonishment. "But you're supposed to read your fortune at the *end* of the meal . . . aren't you?"

"Well, that's the old traditional way," Mark answered, holding out a small hand-painted porcelain bowl that contained two fortune cookies wrapped individually in clear cellophane. "But you know me," he added with a twinkle in his eye, "I like to challenge the old traditions."

Sabrina giggled. "I'm up for it." She reached for

her fortune cookie and tore open the wrapper. "You first."

"Oh, no," Mark said with a mischievous grin. "You read yours first. I insist."

Sabrina shrugged and snapped the crispy crescent-shaped cookie in half, revealing the tiny curled lip of white paper. She pulled it out and quickly read the words. "Ha! At least it doesn't say 'Bad luck will be your shadow' this time."

"What *does* it say?" Mark prompted.

Sabrina chuckled. "It says, 'You will soon travel to a foreign land.' "

"How exciting for you," Mark commented.

"Yeah, right. Except we've got that math test on Monday. So I won't be going anywh—"

Suddenly Sabrina felt the table tremble beneath her fingertips. She could just barely see Mark grinning at her through a veil of Chinese-red smoke that swirled through the room, encircling them like a small tornado. Her ears filled with the roar of a storm, and she felt herself rising from the table.

Why is Mark smiling? Sabrina thought vaguely, right before she felt herself tossed headfirst through the mystical fabric of space and time.

Chapter 10

$\mathcal{S}$abrina landed, hard, on her bottom—without a wonton–and was vaguely aware of several sharp claws clinging to her back through her thin cotton T-shirt.

She buried her face in her hands for a few moments, waiting for her head to stop spinning.

The noise of the storm had been replaced by near silence, interrupted only by the eerie whining of a wind that seemed to come from far off.

Sabrina opened her eyes and looked around. She was sitting on some kind of old bridge with stone walls on either side—no!

She jumped up, ran to the stone wall, looked down, and gasped. It was at least a twenty-foot drop to hard ground—not water. This was not a bridge at all, but some sort of long winding wall with a walkway on top that stretched in both directions as far as the eye could see.

"I have a feeling we're not in Kansas anymore, Dorothy," Salem joked nervously, still clinging tightly to Sabrina's shoulders.

Sabrina nodded. "We're definitely miles from Westbridge—miles from New York City for that matter. But where are we?"

"Beats me," Salem replied. "I never was that good at geography. That's one of the reasons I decided in my past life just to take over the *entire* world. Couldn't keep my countries straight. It made things simpler."

"Uh, Salem," Sabrina said, shrugging her shoulders, "you can let go now."

"Sorry," Salem said. "I have a tendency to cling when I'm being frappéd in blender-force tornado winds." He let go of Sabrina and dropped lightly to the ground. "But just promise me one thing."

"I'll try."

"You won't leave without me?" Salem shuddered. "I don't care what they say about cats, I'm terrible at finding my way home. Especially when the road is one that can only be traveled with a little magic."

"I promise," Sabrina said and gave the cat a reassuring scratch behind the ears. "I just hope I can figure out how to get back."

She walked a few steps, looking around, with Salem dogging her heels. "I don't understand what brought us here—or why. And hey," she whirled around, shielding her eyes against the sun as she looked in both directions, "where's Mark?"

"Not here," Salem said, stating the obvious. "Looks like the spooky red smoke was just meant for you." His long black tail flicked and he scratched the ground. "What's up with that Mark guy, anyway? I thought he liked cats. And you."

"He *does* like cats," Sabrina responded. "He loves them. In fact, he has one of his own named . . ." She stopped in her tracks, and she and Salem stared at each other "Elvis."

"Then how come he called me names and dumped me so rudely out of that chair?" Salem demanded.

Sabrina knew why, and she saw the realization dawn in Salem's bright yellow eyes.

"The fox," they both said at once.

"That wasn't really Mark at all back there in that apartment," Sabrina gasped. "It was Mei the fox posing as Mark! I can't believe I fell for it. I should have known there was no way he would have been there—not unless he were magic, and he's not. And he wouldn't have been mean to you."

"I guess foxes don't care much for cats," Salem said, offended.

"Probably just scared of you," Sabrina reassured her cat. "Now, if only we could figure out—"

Sabrina heard a cough and whirled around.

But it wasn't Mei, as she'd expected. Instead, an old man with a wispy white beard hobbled toward them. The wind ruffled his loose-fitting gray shirt and pants, and he laid a gnarled hand on his wide straw hat to keep the wind from snatching it away.

"Hey! Where'd he come from?" Salem whispered up at Sabrina. "He wasn't here a minute ago."

"I don't know," Sabrina whispered back. "But maybe he can tell us where we are!"

She'd been careful not to reveal her ability to speak Chinese to Mark, but she saw no reason to hide the fact from this old man. She needed answers, and speaking to him in his native dialect would definitely save time.

She said hello in Chinese, and the man answered back.

"Hey, I can't understand you!" Salem hissed.

"Shh!" Sabrina warned him. "A talking cat might scare this guy off, and I need to talk to him."

"Okay, but can you translate?"

Sabrina sighed impatiently, then mumbled a quick spell under her breath:

> *Every word that I say,*
> *Every word that I hear*
> *Let the Chinese be translated*
> *For Salem to hear.*

"It's pretty lame to rhyme the same word," Salem whispered. "Rhyming *hear* with *hear* won't win you any honors in the Witches' Literary Hall of Fame—"

"Hey!" Sabrina whispered back. "You want magic or what? I'll have time to work on my poetry when we get home. *If* we get home!"

Sabrina turned back to the old man. He was staring at her with a puzzled look on his face.

Sabrina laughed nervously. "Uh, excuse me," she said, her Chinese words converted to English for Salem's ears, "but can you tell me where we are?"

The man's white eyebrows shot up. "How can one walk on the Great Wall of China and not know where he is?"

"The Great Wall of China!" Sabrina exclaimed. "You mean, like the great stone wall that extends for one thousand five hundred miles across the northern border of China, which was begun by Emperor Ch'in Shih Huang Ti sometime around 228 BC?"

"Ah, you know Chinese history." The man appeared pleased.

Sabrina shrugged. "My aunt Zelda knows a lot about your country," she explained. "She's always talking about it."

The old man nodded. "China is a good choice if you must soon travel to a foreign land."

"Yes. It's lovely," she said politely, jamming her hands into her pockets, and wondering why his words sounded so familiar. In one of her pockets, her fingers wrapped around a tiny slip of paper, and she absently pulled it out.

The fortune. The one that read: "You will soon travel to a foreign land."

Sabrina's eyes snapped to the old man's face.

"Now that you are here," he said in a cryptic

voice, "you will soon have a showdown with an ancient creature of magic."

"This guy talks like a fortune cookie," Salem whispered to Sabrina.

"Maybe that's because—" Sabrina leaped toward the old man and grabbed him by the hand.

A gnarled hand that seconds later transformed into the soft slender hand of a young girl.

"Mei!" Sabrina exclaimed.

In mere seconds the old man had transformed into the familiar young girl Sabrina knew as Mei. She slipped out of Sabrina's startled grasp and leaped onto the high stone wall.

"Whoa! Wish I could do that!" Salem exclaimed, no longer worrying about hiding his ability to talk before this magical creature.

"Perhaps I could assist you—'you mangy cat!' " Mei replied sweetly. "I would be glad to turn you into something else—say, a tiny cricket? Wouldn't that make a nice meal for a hungry bird?"

Salem hissed as the hair stood up on his back. "Sabrina! Don't let her touch me! Eight inches tall is as short as I can bear to go!"

Sabrina stepped in front of Salem and stared Mei down.

"So the truth comes out," Sabrina said. "I know who you really are. There's only one thing I don't understand."

"What, *Sa-BRI-na!*"

"Why? Why Westbridge? Why me?"

"Why not?" Mei chuckled.

"That's not an answer!"

Mei twirled a strand of her long dark hair in her hand. "I'll tell you why, seeing as how you won't have a chance to tell anyone back in Westbridge."

Sabrina shivered but tried not to show her fear.

"You see, Sabrina, the story Grandmother Chu told you is not a legend or a fable. It is true what she said about me and my kind. The funny thing is, I am a lot like you."

"Like me?" Sabrina exclaimed. "How so?"

"My mother was a magical being—a Chinese fox," Mei explained. She was five hundred years old when she fell in love with my father—a mortal man. So she took on the form of a beautiful young girl and tricked him into marrying her."

"What did he do when he found out?" Sabrina asked.

"He didn't know for a long time," Mei said. "She would stay as a young woman till he went to sleep. Then she would change back into a fox and run through the fields at night, howling at the moon. Then one night, my father followed his young wife and learned what she really was."

"What did he do?"

"At first he was angry. He was going to leave. But then he learned that she was expecting his child. He agreed to stay on one condition. That she always remain in her human form. And that she

97

would raise me the same way. She agreed, and soon afterward, I was born."

"Did she keep her word to your father?" Sabrina asked.

"About half the time," Mei said. "We tried to show only our human sides around my dad, but we often traveled together as foxes." She shrugged. "It's a compromise."

"Sounds like a family *The Jerry Springer Show* would like to get their hands on," Salem whispered.

"Shhh!" Sabrina whispered. "That's a very interesting story," she told Mei. "But what does it have to do with me?"

"Ah, well, my mother happens to know some relatives of yours," Mei said.

"Relatives of mine?" Sabrina exclaimed. "Who?"

"Your Cousin Marigold and Aunt Vesta. Marigold was always gossiping about you, this half-witch, half-mortal teenager—"

"Gee, that's nice to know," Sabrina said.

"And Aunt Vesta was always bragging about you. How, despite your mother's genes, you were a wonderful witch. And how you and your family insist on you learning to live in the mortal world as well as the Other Realm. Well—when my mother told my father about you, they finally agreed on something. They decided that I, too, must have this wonderful mortal education. So they sent me off to be an exchange student in Westbridge, so I could see firsthand how this Sabrina Spellman dealt with the world. I didn't want to go. And I was mad at you for being the cause of all this, so I played tricks on you to make you as miserable as I was."

"That's just plain mean!" Sabrina exclaimed.

"What can I say?" Mei shrugged. "It's what we magic foxes do. Make mischief."

The wind was picking up, and Sabrina brushed the hair from her eyes. "Okay, so you've had your fun. Now how about sending me and Salem home."

Mei began to walk a circle around them. "I don't think so."

"How come?" Sabrina demanded.

But when Mei completed her circle and stopped in front of them, Sabrina began to understand.

Sabrina was staring at a mirror image of herself!

Chapter 11

Hey!" Sabrina shouted. "Give me back my self!"

"I don't think so." Mei ran her hands through her—or rather, Sabrina's—thick blond hair. "You're not as cute as my brunette look, but I think it will be fun to be a blond for a while. Especially when the territory comes with an adorable boyfriend like Harvey."

"You stay away from Harvey!" Sabrina shouted.

Mei giggled. "I know I should. But to be honest, I can't. I have quite a crush on him. You know how teenage girls can be."

"Come on, Salem," Sabrina said, scooping up her cat. "We're leaving." She raised her arms and tried to use her regular magic to send them back to Westbridge.

Nothing happened.

"You got here via my magic," Mei pointed out. "You need me to release that magic in order to get back on your own power."

"Then send us back," Sabrina demanded, "or I'll—"

"Or you'll what? Blast me with some of your witch magic? I don't think so," she said smugly. "Your aunts wouldn't like it. And who knows? Then you might be stuck here forever."

Sabrina was so mad she had to walk away for a minute. "What are we going to do?" she asked Salem.

"I don't know," he replied. "This is a tricky one."

Up ahead they saw a ricksha rolling toward them carrying two women in silk embroidered gowns. Painted parasols protected their faces from the sun. The driver kept his head down, his face shielded from the sun by a wide-brimmed straw hat.

"Need a ride?" one of the women called out to her.

That voice—it was familiar. It was Aunt Zelda! But what were her aunts doing here? Who cares, they were here now and that's all that matters.

Sabrina started to call out, but suddenly she felt a strange nausea pass over her. She dropped to her knees on the ground and closed her eyes.

"Aunt Zelda?" she heard someone cry out. *It sounds like me!* Sabrina thought. She shook her head to clear her mind, then looked up and saw Mei in her Sabrina incarnation running toward her aunts. She threw her arms around them and cried, "Aunt Hilda! Aunt Zelda! I'm so glad you found me. Take me home—and I'll tell you everything!"

"Wait!" Sabrina shouted, running toward the ricksha. "That's not me, that's Mei!" Her aunts looked confused, and she realized what she'd just said sounded kind of mixed up. "What I mean is, that's really Mei, the Chinese fox, disguised to look like *me*, Sabrina. But I'm the *real* Sabrina."

Aunt Hilda and Aunt Zelda stared at her.

"Yeah, good try!" Aunt Hilda laughed.

"What?"

"Come here, dear," Aunt Zelda said to Mei/Sabrina. "Climb in and we'll go."

"No!" Sabrina shouted, then looked at her hands. They were covered with dark brown fur.

"You're looking a little foxy," Salem said in her ear. "And I do *not* mean that as a compliment."

Oh, no. Mei looked like Sabrina. And Sabrina now looked like a fox!

Chapter 12

It's a trick!" Sabrina told her aunts. She pointed at the fake Sabrina sitting in the ricksha with her aunts. "She's really Mei the fox. I'm the real Sabrina."

"She's lying!" Mei/Sabrina shouted. "She's trying to trick you into taking her back to Westbridge so she can take over my life."

"Don't listen to her!" Sabrina cried. "She's the one trying to trick you into taking her back to Westbridge so she can take over my life."

The aunts looked back and forth between the girls, obviously confused, now.

"Salem," Aunt Zelda asked the black cat. "Which one is really our Sabrina?"

"This one," Salem said, standing shoulder to shoulder with Sabrina the fox. "Mei turned her into a fox to confuse you."

"Don't listen to him!" Mei/Sabrina argued. "She put a spell on him to control his thoughts."

"Don't listen to her!" Sabrina the fox and Salem shouted.

"STOP!" Aunt Hilda stood up in the ricksha holding her head and squeezing her eyes shut. "This is too confusing. It's giving me a headache."

Everyone stopped talking.

Hilda sat back down and looked at her sister. "We need a way to prove who's who."

"Ask her some questions," Sabrina the fox suggested.

"Fine," Mei/Sabrina said. "Go ahead."

Aunt Zelda cocked her head. "What's your father's name?"

"Easy, Theodore. But you two call him Ted."

"That's too easy," Sabrina the fox complained.

"Okay, how many times a month do you get to see your mother?" Aunt Zelda asked.

Good one, Aunt Zelda! Sabrina thought. *A trick question. She never got to see her mother.*

"Zero," Mei/Sabrina replied easily. "If I lay eyes on her, she'll turn into a ball of wax."

"Okay, I'm convinced, let's go," Aunt Hilda said.

Sabrina's heart sank. How could she convince them? Obviously Mei had learned a lot about her through her mother gossiping with Cousin Marigold and Aunt Vesta.

Then Sabrina had an idea. A way to outfox the fox!

"Here." Sabrina went over to her backpack and dragged it with her teeth toward the ricksha. "The proof of who's who is inside this bag."

Salem stared curiously at her, but didn't say a word. Aunt Hilda reached down to pick up the bag. She dug around in it a moment, then looked up at Sabrina with a hard stare. "Nothing in here but a bunch of teenager stuff." She turned to Aunt Zelda. "Let's go home."

Salem leaped up on the ricksha and turned sad eyes toward Sabrina. His eyes said, "I don't get it," but for once he kept his mouth shut.

"Oh, wait," Hilda said. She handed Mei/Sabrina a tissue. "You've got a smudge on your cheek."

"Where?"

"There."

"Here?" Mei/Sabrina asked, rubbing at a spot.

"No, there."

"Here?"

"Oh, let me see if I have a mirror." Aunt Hilda dug into Sabrina's backpack and noticed the broken True You Mirror. She quickly fixed it and turned the hand-held gilded mirror into a small compact. "Here."

Without thinking, Mei/Sabrina looked in the compact to check for the smudge—and a dark-haired fox stared back at her.

Both aunts and Salem saw it.

"Eeek!" Mei/Sabrina exclaimed, trying to wiggle her way out of it. "What kind of weird magic mirror is this?"

"A True You mirror," Aunt Zelda said. "A mirror that never lies."

"But that's not me!" she cried.

Sabrina jumped up in the ricksha and looked into the mirror. Her normal face smiled back at her.

Aunt Hilda and Aunt Zelda gave her a hug.

"Sorry we doubted you," Aunt Zelda said. "Can you ever forgive us?"

"You have to admit it was pretty confusing there," Aunt Hilda pointed out.

"I'm just glad we've got it all worked out," Sabrina said.

Mei/Sabrina jumped out of the ricksha and in the blink of a fairy's wing turned back into an original brunette. "This is a much cuter look," she said smugly. "And you're still stuck being a fox. Only I can release you. But I won't, because you spoiled all my fun."

"Oh, yes, you will," said the ricksha driver in heavily accented Chinese as he raised his head.

"Uh, Dad!" Mei exclaimed. "W-what are you doing here?"

"I've come to collect my daughter and take her home," he replied sternly.

"But, Dad, wait, let me explain—"

"You can explain at home," her father replied. "You have embarrassed yourself and your family with your cruel mischief. But you can begin to set things right by releasing Sabrina from your magic."

"Oh, pooh. Do I have to?"

"I'm going to count to five. One . . . two—"

"No, Dad, stop! I hate it when you count!" Mei

pouted, but did as she was told. In two shakes of a fox's tail, Sabrina was back to her normal self.

"Thanks," Sabrina said.

Mei made a face.

"Mei! Say you're welcome! And apologize!"

"You're welcome," Mei said like a sulky child. "And I'm sorry I turned you into a fox—"

"And?" her father prompted.

"*And*—I'm sorry I played all those tricks on you."

"Apology accepted," Sabrina said. No use in holding a grudge, she figured. Dealing with her father's disappointment would be plenty of punishment.

Then Mei's father turned toward Sabrina and her aunts and bowed. "Kids these days!" he muttered under his breath. "Hilda, Zelda, so nice to see you again. Please forgive my daughter. She still has a lot of growing up to do."

"We understand," Aunt Zelda said gently.

"So, can you get home on your own?" he asked. "I have quite a bit of talking to do."

Aunt Zelda nodded. "Come on, girls." She, Hilda, and Sabrina, along with Salem, stepped down out of the ricksha. Mei climbed in, and her father took up the poles.

"Goodbye!" Aunt Zelda called. "And please say hello to your lovely wife for us."

Sabrina gave her aunts a big hug.

"So, where to?" Aunt Zelda asked the group.

"Hong Kong," Aunt Hilda said. "We've got some serious shopping to do."

"Could we stop for a little Chinese food first?" Sabrina begged.

"Yeah," Salem added. "We're sta-a-arving."

"Excellent idea," Aunt Zelda said. "I know a wonderful little place that makes the best dumplings you've ever tasted."

☆

Chapter 13

☆

Sabrina Spellman was late for school.

She'd overslept again, but who wouldn't have after traveling from Westbridge to New York City to China—and back—all in one night. She was still suffering from a terrible case of jet lag.

Fortunately Aunt Zelda had given Sabrina permission to take the witch express to school, so the bell had just begun to ring as she ran down the hall to her locker.

She was actually happy to be back at school. She was looking forward to seeing Harvey again, especially now that Mei the foxy prankster was grounded and wouldn't be setting foot in Westbridge High School for a long time—if ever.

She wasn't sure how she'd explain what happened to Mark. She wasn't sure if he was ready to believe in his grandmother's magic. And she knew that she was going to have to make it clear to him that she liked him very much—as a friend.

"I can't believe her!" she heard Libby complaining loudly to Cee-Cee and Jill as they strode down the hall. "Mei left without a word. And she took my new pair of Italian ankle boots with her! Can you believe the nerve?"

Sabrina chuckled. She had a feeling Libby was never going to see those boots again.

"I can't believe it," she heard someone else say. This time it was Valerie, walking along hugging her books, with her head hanging down.

"Val, are you all right?" Sabrina asked.

"She just left . . ." Valerie said sadly. "Without even saying goodbye."

"Who?" Sabrina asked, even though she guessed she knew.

"Mei." Val sighed. "I thought she was so nice. But I guess she wasn't. Not really. She wasn't a good friend like you."

"Thanks," Sabrina said.

Sighing, Valerie headed toward her first class. "I'll see you at lunch."

Sabrina spun her combination lock, clicked it open, then swung open her locker door.

A small bag of fortune cookies tumbled out.

"Oh, no!" Was Mei back? Sabrina looked around.

No sign of a Chinese fox. But one gorgeous American teenage hunk stood right next to her, smiling.

"Hi, Harvey."

"Hi, Sab." He stared at the bag that had just tumbled from her locker. "Another prank?"

"I . . . I don't know," she said. "I—"

"All right, I confess, it was me this time," Harvey said bashfully. "I know how much you like Chinese food. And I noticed you seemed kind of down lately. I thought a bagful of good-luck fortunes would cheer you up."

"Really? How sweet."

Harvey looked around. "No Mark Wong today?"

"No . . ."

Harvey bit his lip. "Seems like you two have been spending a lot of time together lately."

"We're doing a science project together," she explained.

Harvey's smile came back. "Oh. That's great. Mark's a nice guy."

"Yeah, he is."

"I thought maybe you were avoiding me or something."

"Avoiding *you?*" Sabrina exclaimed. "But you were always busy with Mei."

Harvey frowned. "Yeah, she seemed like a nice girl. But I had no idea how much time it would take when she asked me to show her around town. You know me, I just didn't know how to say no. And then whenever I saw you, you were either with Mark or dashing off like you didn't want to see me."

"But . . ." Sabrina couldn't believe how mixed up things had gotten. She *had* dashed off a lot when she'd seen Harvey with Mei. And she'd spent a lot of time with Mark in the last couple of days. "I promise, I wasn't avoiding you."

"So . . . neither of us was avoiding the other one after all, huh?" Harvey said.

Sabrina grinned. "We'll have to make up for that, won't we?"

"The Slicery? After school?"

"I'll meet you here."

"Hey, and, maybe you can help me with my math homework?" he asked hopefully.

"Sure, if you help me with my Foosball."

"Deal!"

Harvey reached for the bag of fortune cookies and *ri-i-i-ped* open the top.

Down the hall Vice-Principal Kraft stuck his head out the doorway of the office. "I heard that! No snacking in the halls!"

"Sorry, Mr. Kraft. But it's not snacking, it's breakfast," Harvey explained. "Coach's orders."

"Coach's orders?"

Harvey nodded. "Yes, sir. We're trying to bulk up for the game."

"Oh. Well, then. Carry on." He disappeared back into the office. Mr. Kraft was big on school sports.

Harvey chuckled and handed Sabrina a fortune cookie, "Here, have some breakfast. See what it says."

Sabrina tore open the crispy cookie and pulled out the tiny slip of paper. Her fortune read: "Hold on to what you feared was lost."

"What's it say?" Harvey asked.

She showed him the fortune.

Harvey smiled. "Sounds like good advice."

Sabrina stuck the fortune up in her locker, then locked it up.

"Going my way?" Sabrina asked.

"Yep."

Sabrina and Harvey walked each other to class, very, very slowly.

Let Sabrina cast a spell on you in her next magical book . . .

#27 Haunts in the House

Halloween's coming up and what better way to celebrate than with a haunted-house fundraising event. Everyone in Westbridge pitches in including . . . a hobgoblin! Hobgoblin's are great guys to have arorund — they protect your house and like nothing better than helping out in any way they can. But, don't upset them because then . . . they turn nasty! Which is just what Sabrina discovers when Salem goes out of his way to ruin the Hobgoblin's day.

Instead of helping, the hobgoblin reeks havoc and causes chaos galore. And, according to Sabrina's aunts, there isn't the witch born that can match a hobgoblin in sheer magical fury. Gulp. Looks like this could be the scariest Halloween ever!

Gaze in to the future and see what wonders lie in store for
Sabrina, The Teenage Witch

#28 Up, Up and Away

Sabrina and her three mortal friends, Harvey, Valerie and
Libby have blown their science project sky high! They've got
one week to re-do their pathetic project but they're feeling
less than enthusiastic! Luckily for them, before they can get
started, Sabrina finds a puzzle with a spell that transports
them to Paris in 1783. Things go from bad to worse when
the four friends find themselves captive at the hands of a
couple of crazy French hot-air balloonists!

They're determined to break out and it looks like the only
way is up . . . and down — literally — as they do a crash
course in ballooning and learn plenty about science along
the way!

Don't miss out on any of Sabrina's magical antics — conjure up
a book from the past for a truly spellbinding read . . .

#25 While the Cat's Away
Margot Batrae

Imagine if you could have your heart's desire . . . Well, that's just
what happens to Sabrina's cat, Salem, when wizard Drell hits
town. He was going to give his Heart's Desire computer chip to
the teenage witch, but Salem scoffed it before Sabrina even got a
look in. And Salem's heart's desire is . . .? To be human again of
course! Only he forgot to specify that he still wanted to be a
warlock — *not* a mere mortal. Salem's giving Sabrina a run for her
money when he takes the form of a teenage boy and she's got to
play chaperone for him at home and at school. The problem is
Salem's even more trouble as a human than he was as a cat.

Sabrina's got her work cut out trying to convince her feline friend
that really his heart's desire is to go back to his pussy-cat persona
and leave the human touch alone!

No need to feel like you've missed out — have a blast from the past with Sabrina . . . !

#24 Scarabian Nights
Nancy Holder

Aunt Vesta's been to Egypt and instead of bringing Sabrina the usual plastic pyramid, she's brought back an authentic ancient charm as a souvenir. The trouble is, the first time the teenage witch tries to use it to speed up her boring chores — it transports her, Salem and Valerie back in time to ancient Egypt and a whole heap of trouble!

It seems the Egyptians were moggy mad and worshipped their feline friends as gods. Needless to say Salem's lapping it up. But when the Cat Goddess Bast takes a shine to the little fellow it begins to look like his number's up. She locks Sabrina and Valerie inside the Great Pyramid, lost in a maze of mind-numbing complexity, and puts Salem in a love lock so powerful if he doesn't break the spell he could end up seeing out his days as a somewhat crummy mummy.

Time to conjure up some major magic and enlist the help of a handsome young pharaoh to get out of the past, back to the present and still have a future to look forward to!

Keep the magic in your life with a sparkling new Sabrina title out every month!

About the Author

CATHY EAST DUBOWSKI has written many books for children and young adults including *Sabrina, the Teenage Witch* titles *Santa's Little Helper* and *A Dog's Life*. Her husband, Mark, is a writer too and they have even been known to collaborate on some of their books.

Cathy writes in her office in a big red barn in North Carolina, where she lives with Mark, daughters Lauren and Megan, and their two golden retrievers, Macdougal and Morgan.

Nancy Drew™

Nancy Drew — Carolyn Keene — Runaway Bride

Nancy Drew — Carolyn Keene — False Pretences

Nancy Drew — Carolyn Keene — Out of Bounds

Nancy Drew — Carolyn Keene — Making Waves

Nancy Drew — Carolyn Keene — Shadows of Evil

Nancy Drew — Carolyn Keene — Flirting with Danger

Nancy Drew — Carolyn Keene — Fatal Attraction

Nancy Drew — Carolyn Keene — Till Death Do Us Part